# RECKLESS WITH YOU

## SPECIAL THAN

## LESS THAN

## CARRIE ANN RYAN

Reckless With You
A Less Than Novel
By: Carrie Ann Ryan
© 2019 Carrie Ann Ryan
ISBN: 978-1-63695-410-3

Cover Art by Echo Grace

# PRAISE FOR CARRIE ANN RYAN

"Carrie Ann Ryan knows how to pull your heartstrings and make your pulse pound! Her wonderful Redwood Pack series will draw you in and keep you reading long into the night. I can't wait to see what comes next with the new generation, the Talons. Keep them coming, Carrie Ann!" – Lara Adrian, New York Times bestselling author of CRAVE THE NIGHT

"Carrie Ann Ryan never fails to draw readers in with passion, raw sensuality, and characters that pop off the page. Any book by Carrie Ann is an absolute treat." – New York Times Bestselling Author J. Kenner

"With snarky humor, sizzling love scenes, and brilliant, imaginative worldbuilding, The Dante's Circle series reads as if Carrie Ann Ryan peeked at my personal wish list!" – NYT Bestselling Author, Larissa Ione

"Carrie Ann Ryan writes sexy shifters in a world full of passionate happily-ever-afters." – *New York Times* Bestselling Author Vivian Arend

"Carrie Ann's books are sexy with characters you can't help but love from page one. They are heat and heart blended to perfection." *New York Times* Bestselling Author Jayne Rylon

Carrie Ann Ryan's books are wickedly funny and deliciously hot, with plenty of twists to keep you guessing. They'll keep you up all night!" USA Today Bestselling Author Cari Quinn

"Once again, Carrie Ann Ryan knocks the Dante's Circle series out of the park. The queen of hot, sexy, enthralling paranormal romance, Carrie Ann is an author not to miss!" *New York Times* bestselling Author Marie Harte

*To Chelle.*
*Thank you for reminding me.*

# Reckless With Her

From the NYT Bestselling Author of *Breathless With Her* comes a fake relationship romance that's all too real.

Professing her love to her best friend while wearing only her favorite panty set and coat probably wasn't the best decision Amelia Carr has ever made. In fact, it's perhaps the worst. But when her family becomes their overprotective selves while encroaching on her life, she makes a rash decision: her brother's best friend will just have to be her beard. Too bad, he has no idea what he's in for.

Tucker Reinhard loves women, and they tend to love him even more. Despite the love, he *never* would have expected Amelia to come up with the plan she poses to him. He'll go along with it, but only because he doesn't want to see her hurt—even if that means fighting his best friend.

In the midst of her scheme, Amelia realizes she doesn't know Tucker as well as she thought. And neither of them are prepared for what happens when they let the façade go and see what truly lies beneath.

# ONE

*Amelia*

I'M GOOD AT MAKING MISTAKES. AFTER ALL, I'VE had twenty-six years' worth of learning how to make them in spectacular fashion. I'd like to say I'm good at making them with grace and dignity, but that just isn't the case.

I make mistakes. I make them often.

And, sometimes, I realize those mistakes were made for a reason. So I can learn and grow from them.

In retrospect, I can look back on them and figure out exactly what I did wrong. I can figure out what I need to do now and how I can be a better person because of it.

I can become a better Amelia. A better Carr.

But as I'm making the mistake?

Sometimes, it feels like the world is crashing down

around me, and I just want to fall into a hole, bury myself, and never come out.

Sometimes, those mistakes are difficult to figure out, to realize that I'm actually making them, so I make things worse by compounding them with even more mistakes.

But I'm human.

So human that I know we all make bad choices. We think we're doing the right thing, and then suddenly realize that we're not. We screw up to the point where everything is bad, and all we want to do is die. Hide away from the world and forget that those mistakes ever happened.

Sometimes—especially when I was younger—I didn't want to look at those wrong choices I made. I wanted to forget them. Move past them.

Like that time I was in school, and the teacher split up the class into rows facing each other. Three rows on the left side of the room, and three on the right.

That meant I literally faced some of my classmates. On A days, the ones where I actually had that class, I couldn't wear a skirt because that meant facing the rest of the class and...

Everybody could see up your skirt.

I had no idea why our Portuguese teacher decided to set up the room that way. Maybe because she wanted to be able to walk through the classroom as she focused on what we were doing, listening to us annunciating the words horribly.

But it wasn't like I could change any of it. So, I just

didn't wear skirts. Because people who had that class before me had warned me. Like they warned me not to wear a dress on days where we had geography with Mr. Clampton. He liked to put the girls in skirts up front. He was never super creepy about it, never touched, or really even looked. But it wasn't a coincidence that the girls always sat up front.

Mr. Clampton no longer worked at the school, thank God.

Because it wasn't like you actually told your parents that things were creepy. You just relayed to the next generation how things were. And it wasn't until you realized...oh my God, that's actually horrible!...that you took things to the next level and got him out of the school.

But I digress. There was that one time in Portuguese class that I made a mistake. So bad that I was determined not to think about it again. I figured I'd bury it down deep in my subconscious and maybe deal with it later. When I was an adult. You know, after therapy. Because everybody on TV had therapy. So, I mean, I figured I would just deal with it then. I wasn't going to deal with it when I was a fourteen-year-old girl.

Because there was this kid named Lee. Lee was about my height—so a little short for a boy—but I hadn't minded. He was sweet, kind of funny, a little mean, but I didn't mind. Because, sometimes, he paid attention to me. And I was one of those girls.

The ones I hated.

I wanted someone to notice me. So this skinny boy named Lee did this thing with his chair where he would make a circle with his body. He would lean against his legs under the chair and fold himself into a pretzel, then do circles around the desk itself.

He did it over and over, and when the teacher wasn't looking, everyone would try it.

The slender girls would do it, and everyone would laugh. Some of the guys would do it.

Though some of the more muscular guys just scoffed and said, "Hell, no."

I wanted to be one of the cool people. So, I tried.

Notice, I said *tried*.

I tried and got stuck.

Imagine it. My legs are spread, and I'm face-down under the desk, my body stuck between my legs in a folded-up position.

And everyone saw.

Thankfully, I got myself out quickly and just waved it off, my cheeks flaming red as I said, "Yeah, oops." It wasn't until later that I realized it was because I had boobs. And even though I was short and still tiny, boobs got in the way of everything.

I might love them now, but I did *not* love them when I was in school.

See, that was a mistake. One that I buried and only thought of every once in a while. Usually, it was when I was anxious about something else. Or when I was about to go to bed, knowing that I needed to wake up early the next morning. That's when I thought about all of my wrong choices.

Because I hadn't gone to therapy. Instead, I thought about every wrong choice and mistake right when I needed to go to sleep.

Or when I knew that I could possibly make another one.

Like tonight. Tonight, might be a mistake. But I hoped it wouldn't be. I had been waiting for months for this. Years.

Because I knew there was someone I was destined to be with.

While I understood why I didn't truly believe in fate and everlasting happiness and love— you really couldn't in the house I grew up in—I did think that some things were meant to be. Was that fate?

Or was that just a long line of decisions that didn't turn into mistakes?

That was what I needed to worry about.

Because tonight, I was going to make something happen. I wasn't going to wait any longer.

It was all about a boy.

Yes, a boy. One who had been sitting next to Lee in that class, who tried his best to go under the table once and made it happen. One who hadn't laughed when I got stuck.

Instead, he had dropped his book from his desk on

purpose, forcing everyone to look at him, including the teacher.

Everybody soon forgot about the fact that I'd gotten stuck. At least, that's what I told myself.

Because I didn't really want to think about anyone talking about me behind my back. I didn't like it now, and I sure as heck hadn't liked it when I was a teen.

But that boy had been my best friend. He still was.

I actually didn't know when Tobey and I had become best friends. I just remember waking up one day and knowing that he was my best friend.

And the love of my life.

I don't really remember when I fell in love with him either.

He's weirdly always been there, forever a part of me.

And I love him with every ounce of my being.

So, yes, maybe it's cheesy, perhaps it's that fate thing that I told myself I couldn't and shouldn't believe in.

But I loved Tobey.

Tobey McMillan, who, oddly enough, looked a little like Tobey Maguire. At least when the actor was going through that hot stage instead of the awkward one.

Tobey with an E. The Tobey who had always been there for me.

I honestly didn't remember when everything with us started. He'd just shown up one day in like middle school or something. Or was it elementary school?

We shared a lunch in the cafeteria, mostly because I wanted half of his ham and cheese, and he wanted half of my tuna fish.

Why my mother would even think to give me tuna fish, I didn't know. But Tobey had loved it, and we had shared.

After that, we shared lunches until college. I always got one thing, he got another, and we split them.

I never wanted for anything. Never had to wonder what the other side was like because Tobey was there, and I knew he would always share with me.

If I needed help at work, he was there. If I needed help with my math or science homework when we were younger, he was there. I'd helped him with his English and history. And we just learned together.

We were never the type of friends that did things for each other in terms of me doing his homework for him.

Mostly because we wanted to be able to do it ourselves, but it was still nice to know that we always had someone to rely on.

And considering that I had three big brothers who I could also rely on, I knew I was pretty lucky.

No, my parents hadn't been the best, what with all the drinking, cheating, fighting, and yelling.

But it hadn't mattered. Not really.

Because I had my brothers—all three of them in their big, bearded ways. And I had Tobey.

He was sweet, caring, and sometimes a little aloof. Occasionally, he got distracted by things and forgot important details, but he always came through in the end.

I loved him.

We were always the *will they, won't they* couple.

I had dated others in high school and college, of course. And he had dated, as well.

It'd always given me a little clutch of jealousy when he did, but in the end, I realized that it didn't really matter. We could go through life and find our own paths, but in the end, I knew we would end up together.

Because that was fate.

Apparently, I *did* believe in fate. Who knew?

My brothers thought Tobey and I were already dating. After all, we were constantly together. Always touching each other, holding one another, and sometimes even kissing. But only in that quick way, a peck on the cheek, the forehead. Maybe a brush on the lips. As if we had always been together.

Sometimes, we acted like we were an old married couple, and that was fine by me. Because I loved him. But I was also kind of through waiting. Waiting for him to make a move, to tell me that we were ready to take that next step. He'd told me that he loved me. Like I'd said it to him.

Sometimes, a small part of me worried that that love was just friendship—not that there was anything *just* about friendship.

What we had couldn't be altered, not in any irrevocable way. But it could be built upon. And I knew we were ready.

So this wasn't going to be one of those mistakes of my past. It couldn't be. Not when it came to Tobey and me.

But waiting for Tobey to do anything was sort of a lose-lose situation. Because the man worked on his own timetable. He had spent an extra year in college, mostly because it had taken him a while to figure out his major. And then it'd taken him another six months to really figure out what job he wanted once we graduated.

Tobey took forever for most things. I even usually picked out our meals, and he just agreed with it, because if not, it would take forever to decide what we were going to eat. If we wanted to go out for a movie, he usually said, "you pick, Amelia."

Yes, Tobey was a little slow off the start. But that was fine.

I had plenty of decisions inside for both of us. And I was quick at making them.

Maybe that's why I made so many mistakes in the past. But it was fine, because Tobey would be there for me, even if I made more.

Tonight was the night. I was finally going to tell him that I truly loved him. Convince him that we were meant to be together. I was finally ready to do this thing. Waiting for Tobey to actually start this thing between us and take it to the next level? Yeah, no. I wasn't really keen on waiting any longer.

As it was, everyone already considered us a couple. Part of me did, as well. Not the parts that actually had sex, but every other part of me.

We had dinner together most nights, we talked to each other or texted with each other every day.

I had a key to his house, he had mine. He was always helping me with work, and I tried to help him too, but he was a computer scientist and didn't really need my help. I worked with my hands and did more manual labor since I was a landscape architect. I sometimes needed those extra muscles.

And while Tobey had been skinny and a little less muscle-y when he was a kid, he was nicely filled out now.

Tobey was damn sexy. I loved my best friend.

And I couldn't wait to officially tell him.

But because I was me, and I had gotten drunk one night to formulate this plan, I was going to have fun while doing it.

Because we deserved fun.

We had been through a lot recently, mostly thanks to two of my older brothers, so it would be nice for it just to be us. We deserved this.

And with that thought, I looked at myself in the mirror and let out a shaky breath.

"You are fine, Amelia," I told myself. "You are beautiful, busty, lusty, and so ready to get this going."

And...I was never saying *that* statement again. Busty and lusty? Why don't I just read a *Penthouse* magazine and get it on with myself?

Well, considering that what I was about to do might end up as a *Penthouse* Letter to the Editor, I planned to have some fun with it.

I bent down low and lifted my boobs into the cups of my lacy bra so they'd sit just right. It was a deep-plunged bra that had padding at the bottom, not to give me more of my girls—because I had plenty of those—but to lift and separate. It had this thick band below the cups that sort of made it like a corset, but not really. I called it more of a bustier, not that I actually knew what those were. I generally wore whatever bra was the comfiest.

But tonight was all about lace and boob.

I quickly adjusted my lace panties as well, and then grinned. Yes, I was wearing a matching set, and some high heels that I loved. They were the strappy kind so I couldn't walk out of them like I'd done once at that bar, even though I had been sober.

And this was *all* I was going to wear. Well, this and the coat. I didn't actually own a trench coat, and I didn't want to go too far.

So I was wearing my peacoat with all the extra buttons.

This was my outfit for the night.

I was going to show up at Tobey's house, show him his new present, and say, "*You know what? It's time we do this thing.*"

I could be seductive. I had seduced many a man in my time.

Okay, a *few* men, and they mostly did the seducing because I wasn't great at it. But I had been practicing with this mirror long enough that I should be okay.

Tonight was the night I was going to tell my best friend that I loved him. Nothing could go wrong.

Once again, I ignored that little voice in my head that said I was just going to push him to the back of my mind with all my childhood traumas. And then I told myself that was what therapy was for. I should probably work on getting that therapist.

But enough of that. "Okay. Let's do this."

I quickly shut off the lights, grabbed my bag, and got into my car. I didn't live that far from Tobey, and I probably could have walked. But considering that I looked like I was about to go to the street corner and start a new job, I decided to drive. And I was really good about obeying all the laws on the way.

I probably stopped for a little too long at each stop sign, turned on my blinker earlier than needed for each turn, and obeyed all other traffic laws.

But there was no way I was getting pulled over in this getup.

Unease crawled up my spine as I pulled into Tobey's driveway.

Was I making a mistake?

What would happen if he said no? No...that wasn't going to happen. We were totally on the same page. We just needed a little kickstart. And the getup that I was wearing, even as it tightened around my chest, would work to do exactly that. Because it had to.

Tobey was my everything. My forever.

And I was tired of waiting.

I wanted him to love me, to tell me so, and I wanted us to start our new phase. I was tired of the questioning glances and having others wonder, *will they or won't they?*

Because it was going to happen.

He was my best friend. And falling for your best friend was not only my favorite trope in romance, it was also my life.

I'd had enough downs in my life.

This was the time for the ups. I deserved this. *We* deserved this.

I let out a shaky breath and turned off my car.

It all started now.

And I was going to be brave enough to do it.

This was not a mistake.

I grabbed my bag and got out of the car, smiling as I tried to walk up the driveway in my heels. I could totally walk in heels, I could probably even run in them, but I was a little nervous. And because I knew I had to drive this way, I hadn't had a shot of tequila or anything to help me via liquid courage. But that was fine. I didn't need tequila or any other booze.

Because this was right. It was everything.

This was the choice I needed to make.

I rang the doorbell instead of using my key, and Tobey answered quickly, his eyes wide. He looked so warm, so comfy, so...*mine.*

"Hey, I didn't know you were coming over tonight. Aren't you cold in that dress?" he asked, moving out of the way.

I *was* a little cold, and I wasn't wearing a dress, but all the adrenaline running through my system helped. I was fine. I couldn't really feel anything.

Except my love for the person in front of me.

He had a strong jaw and a little piece of hair that kept falling over his face.

He was so beautiful. So *mine.*

This would be perfect.

"So, what's up?" Tobey asked as he looked down at his phone and then stuck it in his back pocket.

He was constantly attached to his cell. But considering that he loved tech, I didn't blame him.

"I have a few things to say. I probably should've written it down and figured exactly what to say first, but I guess I'll just start."

His eyes widened for a moment before he frowned.

"Should I be sitting down for this?" he asked, a little bit of laughter mixed in with the wariness in his eyes.

"Maybe. But...okay. I'm going to do this. Because this is right. It's time."

"Okay, Amelia. What's going on? What's wrong?"

I shook my head. "Nothing's wrong." I really should have written everything down.

"Tobey, we're best friends."

"Yes, we are."

"Let me just talk first. Is that okay?"

"Okay. But do you want to sit down?"

"No. It's fine. Please, let me continue."

"Okay, babe."

*Babe. See? This is right.*

"We've been best friends forever. You're a big part of my world, and I honestly can't picture my life without you. You're everything to me. I've loved you forever."

"I love you too, babe."

Those words wrapped around me, and I couldn't breathe.

"I really love you, Tobey. I know we've been dancing around this forever, so I figured maybe doing something big would push us to that next level. I figured I could do this first."

I quickly undid the buttons of my coat and let it fall to the floor.

His eyes widened for a minute, his gaze raking down my body. I blushed, knowing this was going to work.

Tobey liked big moves. He was one of those people that did things in flashes, even if he was quiet about it sometimes.

This was going to work.

But when his gaze met mine, something broke inside of me.

My skin pebbled, but not from what I wanted it to.

No, it was the sheer mortification sliding through me. Because he wasn't moving forward, he wasn't looking at me with hunger or love in his gaze.

No, there was horror there. Confusion.

And maybe a little pity.

How? How had I misread the situation?

"Babe?"

I quickly reached down and put my coat on.

"Okay, so that was a little fast. Maybe I shouldn't just show you the goods at first. Forget that happened. But we should talk."

"Yeah, I think we should. Babe, I love you. But I don't love you like that."

I didn't know the sound of a heart breaking could actually echo in your ears. It sounded like a gunshot, one ricocheting through my body as it shattered my organ into a thousand pieces. Acid pooled in my gut, and my head ached as I tried to comprehend exactly what he'd said.

*I don't love you like that.*

Like...that.

Like I loved him.

This was a mistake.

One that I had talked myself out of. Something that I would try to bury in the back of my mind and forget. Because there was no way I could live through this without making another one.

"Babe."

"Why don't you stop calling me *babe.*" I said it softly, my voice wooden.

I had just shown my boobs to my best friend, and he didn't love me.

He wasn't even moving towards me. No, his hands were in his pockets, sorrow on his face.

And that damned pity.

"I can do that, Amelia. But there's something I should tell you."

"I think you've said enough. Well, at least *I* said enough for both of us."

I tried to move past him, but he reached out and grabbed my arm. I didn't mean to flinch. I think the fact that I did shocked both of us. I moved away, tightening my jacket around myself, wishing I could just fall into a hole and never come out.

"I'm dating someone, Amelia."

My gaze shot to his. "Dating?" Tobey was dating? We talked *every day*, and he'd never mentioned it before.

*Oh my God. What have I done?*

"Yeah. I love her, Amelia. I think I've found my forever with her. I didn't know how to tell you before."

"You love her. Your forever?"

"Yeah. And one day, I hope you get to meet her. I just... I'm sorry Amelia. I should have told you."

I looked at him then and raised my chin. I wasn't going to cry. I couldn't cry in front of my best friend. Not even when I was breaking inside. I would simply raise my chin even higher. And nod.

"Yeah. You should have."

And then I ran.

I had just told my best friend that I loved him. And found out that he didn't love me back.

There was no coming back from that.

# Two

*Tucker*

"EXCUSE ME, DO YOU THINK YOU COULD HELP ME reach that zucchini?"

I looked over at the woman next to me in the grocery store and nodded, giving her a small smile. Then I got a look at her face.

Picking up women in the grocery store wasn't something I generally did, and since I had plans that night, I wasn't going to do much tonight either, but I could still appreciate the woman with the thick curves and plump lips at my side.

I couldn't help it.

I liked women. And women tended to like me, which I didn't mind. Not at all.

"Sure, what size are you looking for?"

I held back a mental groan because I hadn't actually meant to sound like I was thinking about my dick. But from the way she blushed, and the fact that her gaze raked down my body before moving back to my eyes? Yeah, she got the double entendre.

Oops.

"Well, I kind of wanted one a little bigger. Does that work for you?"

Dear God, I was somehow in the middle of a porn movie. And me, without my tripod.

I really needed to stop with the jokes. I wasn't very good at them.

"I'll see what I can do for you." I winked and looked at the zucchini, finding one that didn't actually look as phallic as the rest. Because what if I was reading the situation wrong? What if she really did just want a nice zucchini for her family? One that was large enough to feed them all.

One that did not remind her of my dick.

But when she pressed closer to me, her breasts tight against my side, I had a feeling she was thinking about dick, too.

Oh, good. I had reached the stage of my life where I could make zucchini dick jokes no matter what I was doing.

Okay, I had to be honest with myself, I could always make a dick joke. It was kind of my thing.

"Here you go."

"Oh, and it's so...firm."

She winked, and I held back a groan.

Really? Really? There were kids all around us, and she was squeezing that zucchini in a way that made me want to cross my legs. Because given how she squeezed, it made me wonder how she'd squeeze my junk.

Her next words broke me out of my thoughts. "Anyway, thank you."

"You're welcome. Now, if you'll excuse me, I have to go look at that artichoke over there."

I hurried off, aware that she was watching my ass as I moved away. I hadn't actually done that on purpose, but whatever. That had been a little too strange for me. When another lady came up to her, and they both started giggling, pointing, and watching me, I had to wonder if I was on some candid camera TV show that I wasn't aware actually existed anymore.

I knew women were drawn to me. Men, too. And, sometimes, I used it to my advantage. Other times, I ignored it. They liked the way I looked, liked my smile, my muscles. They just liked what they saw.

I could be charming. I had been a charmer when I was younger, after all. That's how I'd charmed myself from foster home to foster home. I had charmed my way through all of them until I found the perfect one that I could stay at until I was eighteen. One where no one touched me when I didn't want them to. Where no one hit me or yelled. They were a good family. One that probably thought fondly of me every once in a while but didn't necessarily remember me.

The perfect foster family.

But I had used my dimples and that smile of mine to get what I wanted. And I hadn't been ashamed of it. Foster kids had to learn young. It was sort of our thing.

And so, I used that *swerve* of mine—as the kids today said, at least I thought that was what the kids said these days—to get through life.

Tonight, I had plans with the family of my heart, so picking up a lady in the grocery store who fondled zucchini as if it were the last vegetable she'd ever be able to grope, really wasn't on my agenda.

I passed the artichokes and left the produce area, headed towards the flower area like I had planned all along. I wanted to bring a bouquet or something sweet for my best friend's new lady love. Yes, I had lied to the zucchini lady about my need for artichokes, but I hadn't wanted to walk away without saying something. I probably should have said, "*flowers.*" Or that I was busy. Maybe I shouldn't have said anything. But no, instead, I had lied.

And now I felt like an ass.

It didn't matter, though. I wouldn't see her again. This wasn't even my normal grocery store.

I sifted through the flowers until I found a happy bouquet of daisies that had little sprigs of white in them. I had no idea what kind of flowers they were. I usually went with lilies or roses or daisies. Though I knew what tulips were, too.

Devin's little sister, Amelia, would probably know what these are. As would our other friend, Zoey. Considering that Zoey was a florist, and Amelia was a landscape architect, they should know their flowers.

I froze and looked down at the daisies in my hand. Dear God. If I showed up with grocery store flowers, Zoey would probably kill me.

However, her place was closed, so she would just have to deal with it.

Maybe I would buy her some wine or something to make her feel better. Yes, wine. I quickly perused the selection in the wine aisle, grateful that I could actually buy wine at the grocery store. I had visited a state earlier this month where you couldn't buy wine at the grocery store. Why would anyone allow that to happen? What kind of horribleness existed in the world?

And now I was losing it. I was working too hard, and I really needed a break. Hanging out with my found family tonight would be exactly what I needed.

I quickly picked a red and a white, knowing they weren't the best wines out there, but they would be tasty. You could find a really nice twenty-dollar bottle of wine these days.

I paid for my purchases, quickly walking past the

zucchini lady, who was also checking out, without saying anything.

It might have made me an ass, but she was still staring at my ass, so...whatever.

I put the wine in the back seat of my SUV and tossed the flowers onto the front seat. I winced, made sure I hadn't broken any of the petals or stems, and started my engine.

I'd had a long day working at the hospital, and all I really wanted to do was go to bed. I was going to hang out with the Carrs instead.

I had known Devin for years. Since high school. We'd become friends quickly, and had even gone to college together. I'd ended up having to stay in college a bit longer, considering that becoming a diagnostic radiologist meant I needed a little more training than I'd planned on when I started school. But I loved my job.

I loved trying to figure out what made someone hurt. Because I wanted to be able to fix it. Without me, doctors couldn't do their jobs, and nurses would be strained even more than they already were.

I saw things that broke my heart, but then I also saw the strength of humanity that came from that heartbreak. I saw the connections that came from others as they pulled together when their loved one was fighting or in pain.

I saw that people didn't always walk away when things got hard. Sometimes, I got to see them when they were healthy. When it was just a checkup.

I got to see the life shine through their eyes. Something I didn't always get to notice.

And, throughout it all, I noticed the ones with the big families first. Because they were the ones that drew me in. I'd always wanted that. The type of family that would always be there for you no matter what happened. I hadn't had that as a kid. My final foster family had been wonderful. But we didn't talk, didn't chat. They didn't send birthday cards. They did send emails every once in a while, but we weren't that close. Plus, they had other kids who came in and out of their lives. They never adopted, but they were always there for kids in need.

And I was fine with that. I didn't need more because I had Devin and his siblings.

And considering that Devin had gone through his own little version of hell with his parents, it was nice having him. We could lean on each other.

And I liked the fact that we had each other, no matter what.

I pulled in behind Amelia's car in front of Devin's house and grinned.

I liked Amelia. She was sweet, a little feisty, and always had an opinion—especially about me. I didn't mind. If Devin was going to have any kind of little sister, Amelia was the good kind. She had the biggest heart ever. And even when you somehow found yourself covered in dirt and helping her when you didn't even realize you had agreed to it, it was good.

It was that smile of hers. You simply nodded and followed what she said.

Of course, I sort of did the same things sometimes. According to Amelia, it was my dimples.

I couldn't help it. As I said, I liked women. And if I were allowed to look at Amelia that way, I probably would have found her hot. Sweet. Would have loved that smile of hers. Those big eyes. The way she filled out her dresses. And even more, the way she filled out her jeans while she was working. Because those legs of hers? Damn. You could tell that she worked with her whole body. Daily.

I turned off my car and cleared my throat, adjusting myself in my pants.

Well, that was interesting. I hadn't thought about Amelia that way in a while. I wasn't supposed to. She was my best friend's little sister. There were rules about that. Books and encyclopedias and instruction manuals written on how not to think that your best friend's baby sister was hot.

Plus, she was like eight years younger. It wasn't even until recently that I allowed myself to look at her like that at all. Not that I was actually allowed to do it, but at least now the age difference wasn't a big thing.

Not that it should matter since I didn't think of her that way. She was like a sister to me.

No, I wasn't even going to lie to myself like that. There was nothing sisterly about Amelia Carr.

I could think she was hot as fuck, sweet as sin, and just an amazing person, but I wasn't allowed to think about her as anything more than that. Nor was I allowed to let Devin know that I thought about her in that way. Well, Devin and Amelia's two other brothers, as well. Dimitri and Caleb could kick my ass. Oh, Devin could too, but he might hold back his punches a bit because we were best friends. But Caleb? Yeah, while Caleb had never been to prison, at least that I knew of, he could probably break me.

And while their older brother Dimitri might teach kids, I swore there was something rumbling under that nice-guy exterior. He could snap me like a twig.

So, no thank you. I was not going to think about Amelia that way.

Much.

I grabbed my goods and headed towards Devin's door.

Erin answered, her blond hair piled on top of her head in some weird twisty, curled topknot thing. I liked it.

She grinned widely and held out her hands. "Hey there, Tucker. You're here."

"Hey. When are you going to finally leave him and run away with me?" I asked as I leaned forward and kissed her directly on the mouth.

She threw back her head and laughed as Devin scowled at me.

Yeah, kissing the love of my best friend's life without even taking my first step into his house, right after thinking dirty thoughts about his little sister...? Probably not the best move. But I couldn't help it. I loved Erin. She was good for Devin. I liked seeing the two of them moving towards the next phase of their relationship.

They weren't married yet, but I knew that was coming soon. Considering that Erin had already been married once and had been through a hellacious divorce, I was surprised that she was willing to get married again at all. But for Devin? I figured she'd do it.

Not that I ever planned to get married. No, thanks. Watching my friends fall in love and get married was great. But I didn't want any of that. I liked where I was. I didn't want kids, didn't want to get married. I wanted to live my life and be with the family I had.

Anything more could only lead to heartbreak. You could lose it with one snap of the fingers, and I didn't want that. No thanks. Never again.

"Are you done making out with my woman?" Devin asked, and I just smiled. "Hey. I can't help it if you've completely bamboozled her."

"Bamboozled?" Caleb asked, scoffing into his beer. "That's not even a word."

"I'm pretty sure it was a game in that TV show *Friends*," Amelia said, playing with the ice in her glass. She wasn't looking at me. In fact, she was glaring down at her glass of soda, and I had to wonder what the hell was wrong with her. She was usually the one bouncing around, making sure that everyone was fed, or at least had cheese.

There was a cheese joke running around the family. I didn't really know where it had come from, but ever since the eldest sibling, Dimitri, had married Thea Montgomery, there seemed to be cheese all the time. Even when Thea and Dimitri weren't in attendance.

"Yes, but it's actually a word, too." Zoey sidled up and took the flowers from me as Erin grabbed the wine from my other hand.

"Hey there," Zoey said and then reached up to kiss my cheek. "Well, hello there," I crooned. "I'm liking this kind of welcome."

Caleb glowered at me as Devin had, and I grinned.

I loved when things got interesting.

"So, what are we having for dinner tonight?" I asked, tapping my stomach with the palm of my hand. "I'm starved."

"Did you eat anything today while working?" Erin asked. She handed over a beer, and I nodded in appreciation before taking a deep sip. I was thirsty, and Devin always had good beer on hand.

"I ate something."

"Yeah, whatever was from the vending machine?" Devin asked, shaking his head. He leaned on his cane, and I winced. Devin was still healing from when he had gotten hit by a freaking car while on duty. Devin worked long hours as a mailman—or, I'm sorry, a *postal worker*—and had gotten hit by a car while saving a dog. The fact that Devin had issues with dogs and was a little afraid of them in general made what had happened a bit of a surprise. But Devin had a big heart. And, apparently, a thick skull, because he was fine. Minus his spleen, and healing from a broken leg, but he was almost fully back. He only used the cane when he got tired. That way, he could heal quicker. He wanted his route back, and I didn't blame him. I hated when my life got knocked out of sorts by things out of my control.

It was good that things were getting back to normal around here.

At least, I thought it was normal. I looked around and almost opened my mouth to ask where Tobey was, but then I saw Amelia's lowered shoulders and the fact that she still hadn't really spoken to me. Or even looked at me. In fact, everyone seemed to be trying really hard not to look at her.

I looked over at Devin, thankful that Amelia wasn't looking my way, and mouthed the words, "*Where's Tobey?*"

Devin winced and shook his head. My brows rose.

"Okay, for dinner tonight, we made brisket with mashed potatoes, corn, macaroni and cheese, and we have lemon meringue pie for dessert." Erin spoke quickly, and my stomach growled.

"Good God. Do you realize how much I'm going to have to work out to burn all of that off?"

"I think you'll be fine," Zoey said, tapping my abs. I watched how Caleb was curiously *not* looking at her.

Was I just seeing things? No, that couldn't be. Caleb and Zoey had never dated. I was pretty sure they had never even thought about it. Right? Dear God, was I working so much that I had lost my ability to figure out what was going on in my circle of friends? With my family?

I knew that Tobey and Amelia were best friends, and he was always with her. In fact, I was pretty sure they were dating—or at least screwing. However, the fact that she looked like her heart was broken right now, and nobody was talking about it worried me.

Did I have to kick Tobey's ass? Because I could kick his fucking ass if I had to.

And now Caleb and Zoey? Maybe I was just seeing things. Or maybe all that zucchini talk at the grocery store had screwed with my brain.

"Our friend made me a smoker." I looked over at Devin, and my eyes widened.

"Laney's dad?"

"Yep. Made me a smoker because he was practicing his welding or some shit. He made one for Laney and Greg too. So, we have a smoker, and we've been playing around with it. It smells amazing, but if the brisket isn't juicy, let me know."

"You want me to tell you if something's juicy or not?" I asked, lowering my voice.

"Oh, dear God, you have like the dirtiest mind ever," Amelia snapped and then blushed as I looked at her.

"I know. I kind of like it that way. Though you're usually the one with the dick jokes."

She just shrugged and went back to looking at her soda. I looked at everyone else.

What the hell was going on?

Everybody went to set the table, but Amelia stayed at the island bar, looking at her drink.

I moved to her and took the seat next to her.

"You want to tell me what's up?" I whispered.

"Not particularly."

"Everyone's purposely not talking to you or about you. And I know that you hate things like that."

"They're not letting me have any alcohol either. Apparently, they're afraid I'll drown my sorrows in booze or something." She sounded so sarcastic and pained when she said it, I looked around. And found the bottle of whiskey on the counter.

I met her gaze, and she grinned at me, life in her eyes for the first time since I'd walked in.

"I've got you, baby girl."

"At least someone does," she mumbled. My brows shot straight up.

Okay, I needed to get the details out of her. At least, eventually. Though I wasn't going to do it tonight. Tonight, I would pour her a shot or three of her favorite whiskey, make sure it was mixed into the Coke so not everybody would know, and then ensure that she got home okay.

Because this was my best friend's baby sister. And if someone had hurt her, I was going to kick his or her ass.

I had a feeling that since Tobey wasn't here, and Devin was purposely not saying a damn thing about it, something had happened.

One thing was clear. If you messed with Amelia, you messed with all of us.

# THREE

*Amelia*

"HE'S A TWAT," ZOEY SAID, AND I RAISED MY brows at her.

"Why did you say 'twat' in a Scottish accent like that?" I asked, looking down at my single glass of wine. I hadn't even taken a sip yet. All I wanted to do was drown my sorrows and try to pretend that everything was okay. Except it totally wasn't okay. And I had no idea what to do. However, Zoey and Erin were at my house tonight, trying to make sure that I was all right. Not that I thought I'd ever be fine again. Because I was an idiot. A horrible, stupid idiot that had probably lost her best friend forever because I showed him my boobs.

Well, I didn't show him all of my boobs, but enough.

And plenty of the rest of my body. Dear God, I had shown him some of my cellulite. Yeah, I had cellulite. I had curves. Probably a mole or two on my back. And I had shown him all of it.

More than a bathing suit anyway. The lace of my bra had barely covered my nipples. And I had very large nipples.

Oh, God. I was going to die. My heart was going to give out, and then everything would just be better. Because that was the only way I was going to make it through this. I hadn't heard from Tobey, and now, he knew what I looked like practically naked. I had come on to him.

And he loved someone else. He had someone else. Dear God.

"I didn't say it Scottish?" Zoey said, and even though it had begun as a statement, she had sort of ended it as a question.

"Totally in a Scottish accent," Erin added.

"Oh, well, I was watching this video of these two Scottish women in a car, trying to get through some flooding, and this truck drove past really quickly and made things even worse for everyone. So, anyway, one of the ladies in the car started screaming 'twat' at the guy. In a very thick Scottish brogue."

"Well, that would do it. Do women have brogues, or is it only men in kilts on romance novels?" I asked, still looking at my wine. Maybe if I kept looking at it, it would make everything better.

*Spoiler*: it wasn't going to make everything better.

"I don't really know. I've never really thought about it. It's usually just the word *accent* that you use. But *brogue* sounds so sexy when it comes to Scottish." Zoey grinned, shaking her head. "And I didn't really get a look at the Scottish women. They could have been sexy."

"Didn't you date a Scottish woman once?" I asked, grinning.

It wasn't really a grin, more like a smile that didn't reach my eyes. Or maybe one of those manic ones that said everything was okay, that I wouldn't have to throw myself off a bridge so I didn't feel like this anymore.

"Yes, for like a day." Zoey grinned. "She was nice, but we didn't fit time-wise. Her brother asked me out too, but I don't date siblings." As my friend didn't tend to date at all, that was saying something.

"Did she make you eat haggis?" Erin asked, sounding far too innocent. There was nothing innocent about Erin. She was dating my brother. I knew things.

Too many things.

Things I did not want to know. Ever.

"No, I tried haggis on my own."

Erin shuddered, and I snorted.

"We went to that pub and tried a bite of it. It wasn't that bad," I said. Erin looked at me aghast.

"What?" I asked and then looked down at my wine.

Nope, still had problems. Maybe I should actually drink it.

"Haggis. Gross."

"Anyway, before we go off on a Scottish tangent, and we're just going to say *accent* for now and only think of *brogue* when we're talking about Scots in kilts in historical times..."

"Okay, if that's what helps you sleep at night," Erin said, laughing.

"Thank you. I'm going to have great dreams tonight, thinking about hot Scottish men in kilts. And only kilts." Zoey sighed with an overdramatic, dreamy sound, and I knew she was trying to make jokes to make me laugh. But it would be hard to get me to laugh right then. And I hated myself a little bit for it. Because it was totally my fault. All my fault.

"Anyway. Tobey is a twat."

"You're going to make me get a t-shirt that says that, aren't you?" I asked, looking between my friends.

"Definitely," they said at the same time, then looked at each other and laughed.

"And he isn't a twat. *I* was the twat." I looked down at my glass and finally took a big sip. Okay, it was a gulp. Actually, it was like three-quarters of the glass.

Erin gave me a sad smile and then refilled the glass.

I really had true friends here. They didn't even have to ask, and they didn't judge when they filled my glass.

"Tobey is a twat, not you," Erin said. "And I'm not going to say *twat* any more. Except for just then. Regardless, he was an idiot. A jerk. And he was mean."

"How was he mean?" I asked, being truly honest with myself. "How is saying he doesn't love me mean? I get it. He doesn't have to love me. Just because I fell in love with him and thought I was *in* love with my best friend, even though there was clearly nothing between us like that, doesn't mean he's a horrible person. It simply means I need to read signals better. And not try to do the big moments. Because that was stupid. Oh my God, that was so stupid." I buried my head in my hands and tried not to picture it.

But I couldn't help it. It kept replaying in my mind. I knew this was going to be another of those things like the chair incident in school all over again, where all I ever did was think about it when I tried to sleep. Or like if I ever saw my life flash before my eyes if I got into an accident. Or if I was just nervous about something, it would be what came to mind to worry me. Always. No matter what. This is what I would think about now.

And there was no turning back from it.

"Okay, I see where you're coming from. But we are going to break that down a bit," Zoey said, and Erin nodded quickly.

"First," Erin said, "I know about idiots. I married one."

"You can't compare your ex-husband to Tobey."

"No, I can't. But there are some similarities. Things we can get into."

"And let me tell you, we wrote down lists and color-coordinated them and everything. Then we left them behind because we didn't want to seem like we were actually trying to come at you. But here we are," Zoey added.

"Oh. So, is this like an intervention or something?" I gulped more wine and then switched to water. I didn't really want to get drunk in front of them. I would end up crying. Or weeping. Or throwing myself at their feet, wishing they could fix everything and make it all go away. But there was no fixing this. There was no making it go away. It would always be there. Like a mole that couldn't be removed.

My shame. My mistakes.

And, dear God, apparently, I was great at making them.

"He didn't tell you that he was dating anyone," Erin said quickly. "What the fuck is that about?"

"I don't know, maybe he wanted to make it special or something?" I looked down at my hands. I felt like I was watching myself make one horrible decision after another. Why hadn't he told me? Why did I have such a deep ache inside of me, as if something were tearing at me from the inside out?

"He didn't tell you." Zoey shook her head and sipped her wine. "Why? Was he hiding it from you? Yeah, maybe he wanted to keep some things to himself, and I get that. We don't need to tell our best friends everything. But someone that's going to be in a relationship with him, that he's going to state flat-out could be his forever? Someone he really cares about. The fact that he said he found his forever or some shit like that? No, he needed to tell you that. You guys used to tell each other everything."

"Not everything. I didn't tell him that I loved him."

"Well, you did in the end. And the fact that he couldn't see that all along? That's some shit right there. He must have seen *something*."

"Meaning you all saw it?" I asked, sheer mortification sliding over me like a second skin. One that was suffocating.

"You know we did, baby," Erin said, reaching out to grip my hand. "We love you."

"Yeah. But, apparently, I'm a loser who loves somebody that doesn't love me back."

"Well, we could talk about how I feel about that, but we're not going to," Zoey said quickly, and I ignored that. We weren't going to get into Zoey's lack of love life, because then we'd all wind up drinking. Plus, I knew my friend was hurting. Maybe we all were. Erin had been hurting, too. After all, she had walked in on her husband sleeping with another woman. Well, more like banging in a bathroom, but whatever.

But now Erin was happy and in love and in a relation-ship with my brother.

Even my oldest brother Dimitri had been through a

really nasty divorce, one that had actually ended in bloodshed. But I digress.

He was happy in another marriage now, and he and Thea were practically dancing on clouds with gumdrops and rainbows.

Everybody was happy. Well, maybe not everybody, but the current dark cloud was right over my head at the moment, and it was all of my own making.

"I just don't understand why he didn't talk to you about it. If this person is so important to him, they should have shared something. Because you're important to him, too." Zoey looked at me, and I sighed.

"I thought I was. I don't know what any of it means."

"We don't either. And that's why he's a twat." Zoey winced, looked at Erin, and then added quickly, "Or a jerk. Or a loser. I don't know, enter whatever word you want there. Something that states he hid something pretty big. So big, that I feel like he was hiding it on purpose. As in he didn't want her to know about you."

"Or worse, maybe she knew about you, and he didn't want to have to deal with the two of you meeting. After all, not everybody can deal with male and female relationships like that."

"It was an issue a couple of times in the past when Tobey was dating someone, and even when I dated someone. But not on our end. We always made it work."

It probably helped that I was partially in love with

Tobey even then. Or, at least what I thought was love. Maybe I had been wrong about that feeling. I honestly didn't know any more. And the fact that I was questioning everything hurt. I really was tired. Maybe wine would make it better. At least, for the evening.

"I don't know, but it was all a little shady," Zoey said quickly. "Shady enough that we need to rethink everything. I hate what he's done to you. I hate that I can see the doubt in your eyes, and the pain. Yeah, you decided to tell him about your feelings in a fun way, something that should have been very fun, but that's fine. We legit all thought you were dating anyway."

"We weren't."

"I thought you were," Erin said quickly. "And I'm the newest one to the group. Sure, I've known you for a bit, but we were never as close as we've gotten recently. And we all swore you two were dating. Or maybe that you had been dating and broke up or something. But every single one of us thought you guys had at least been together at some point. Or were still. I thought I saw love there, emotion. Something. So, you weren't just making things up in your head. We all saw it. And Tobey relied on you for so much. He was always there for you. And you were legit always there for him."

"That's what friends do."

"Yeah, but not like you two were. You guys were practically an old married couple," Zoey added. "So, yeah, not sure what the fuck he was thinking, but...we love you. And we're sorry that he was an asshole. But you don't get to beat yourself up any more. Okay?"

"Okay," I lied.

They all knew it was a lie, but they let it go. They each stood up and hugged me, and I smiled.

"We'll make it work. He can still be my friend." I heard the desperation in my voice, and the girls pointedly didn't look at each other as they nodded slowly.

"Of course, baby."

I heard the pity in Erin's tone, even though I knew she was trying to hide it.

"Of course."

Tobey had to still be my friend. I couldn't handle it if I'd ruined that, too.

I walked the girls out and then took off my pants.

I did not want to wear pants. Pants should not be required, at least in your own home.

I put away the wine and then took out the Don Julio. I did two shots in a row, no need for lime with the good tequila. And then I turned on my music.

Alanis Morissette would get me through this.

She was the only one that could. After all, *Jagged Little Pill* is an anthem. I might have been too young to really understand it when it first came out, but it was still an anthem.

I blared the music, did another shot, and started

dancing in my underwear. After all, when was a better time to dance in your underwear than when your heart was breaking, and your whole world was shattering?

Because I hadn't heard from Tobey. He hadn't answered my texts or my calls.

And I had sent and placed two of each. And I knew that sounded desperate.

I was so mortified. So afraid to see him again. But I also needed to see him because I had to make sure everything was okay. He was such a big part of my life. I couldn't lose him.

I loved him. But he didn't love me. He loved *her*.

The tequila mixed with my emotions, and I knew I was going crazy, but I didn't care.

"Would she go down on you in a theater, Tobey? Would she? Would she?" I screamed the words, danced and thrashed my head around. I cried out, shaking my ass and dancing around the house.

When the music suddenly stopped and a throat cleared, I froze.

"Please don't be Tobey, please don't be Tobey, please don't be Tobey," I mumbled under my breath.

"Not Tobey," a deep voice said. I turned on my heel, my eyes wide.

"How the fuck did you get in my house?" I screamed at Tucker.

That's when I realized that I had been screaming to

Alanis Morissette while holding the tequila bottle and dancing in my underwear.

Oh, good. Another man who's seen me in my underwear at one of the worst times. I should start creating a spreadsheet to track this. Maybe keep a journal.

Perhaps it could even be my thing—embarrassing myself in my underwear in front of people.

"You left the door partially open, babe."

"I'm not your babe." I burped and then sipped another sip of tequila straight from the bottle. I wasn't a hundred percent sure exactly where I was on my drinking, but considering that I could see two Tuckers in front of me, I had a feeling I'd had more than enough.

"And I did not," I said, snorting.

Ha, I was funny. So funny. But neither Tucker was laughing. Instead, they had their hands in their pockets and were just looking at me.

You know, Tucker looked kind of hot. In a big brother's best friend sort of way. But those thoughts were taboo.

But that wasn't my thing. My thing was falling in love with my best friend.

But that hadn't worked out, had it?

Suddenly, Tucker was in front of me, the bottle of tequila ripped from my hands, and I was leaning on him.

"Hey, stop copping a feel."

"You're mumbling, and I think you said, 'don't cop a feel,' and I'm not. My hands are on your waist, and you're leaning on me only because you were starting to sway so far to the side that you were at a forty-five-degree angle."

"Was not."

"Considering that you hiccupped that, I'm going to say 'were, too.'" He kissed the top of my head, and I sighed, closing my eyes.

"You smell nice."

"I know I do. I just showered."

I took a big sniff. "Why?"

"Because I was working out late at the gym and decided not to get in my car completely sweaty?"

Was totally not going to think about Tucker working out. All sweaty. Just saying.

"Why are you here, Tucker?"

"I wanted to check on you. And I'm glad I did, considering you were dancing around in your underwear with your windows open, the lights on, and your door unlocked and ajar."

"Oh, God," I said, still leaning into him with my eyes closed.

"Yeah, oh God. The girls left you like this?"

"Not really. But I don't really remember." My stomach gurgled, and I groaned.

"Okay, baby, let's sober you up and tuck you into bed."

"I'm not going to bed with you, Tucker. First, *ew*. Second, Devin would kill you. And maybe me."

"I'm a little worried that *ew* was your first thing."

I tried to take a step and teetered. Tucker sighed and put one arm beneath my knees, the other under my shoulders. Suddenly, I was airborne, wrapped around him. My anchor.

"Hey, when did you get so strong?" I tapped his chest, his very *nice* chest, and purred.

Did I just purr?

Oh, God. Apparently, I was really good at embarrassing myself.

"Okay, enough of that." I knew he was muttering to himself, but I could hear him. At least, I thought I could. I wasn't a hundred percent sure about anything anymore.

My stomach gurgled again. This time, I slapped my hand over my mouth.

Tucker cursed under his breath, put the tequila on the counter, and ran me to the bathroom.

I was on my hands and knees in front of him a moment later, and not in a fun way. Not that it was going to be fun with Tucker ever. After all...*ew*.

When did I start saying 'ew?' I wasn't twelve. Dear God, tequila made everything worse.

Tucker's hands were in my hair, though again, not in a fun way. He pulled it back from my face and rubbed his other hand down my back as I threw up in the toilet.

Oh, good, that mortification thing was back. This was a disaster. Another of my own making. What was wrong with me?

I threw up everything I'd just drunk and eaten.

Including the lovely cheese that Zoey had brought over.

God, I couldn't believe I had wasted cheese. And good tequila.

If you're going to throw up anything, it should be rum. Rum is what you threw up.

At least, that's what I had learned.

It probably didn't help that, you know, Dad was an alcoholic and drank a lot. But I had learned all my drinking from him.

And...good. There came that horror. The shame again.

I didn't want to drink my worries away. I knew it didn't help. After all, it certainly hadn't worked for dear old Dad. And it wouldn't work for me. I wasn't going to do this again. I couldn't.

"I hate this," I whispered, tears streaming down my face.

Tucker was in front of me then, pulling my hair into a band behind my head and wiping my face with a washcloth. He was so good at taking care of people. He always had been.

I knew he hadn't really had anyone to take care of him, at least that's what I had gleaned from listening in on conversations over the years. He didn't have anyone now either. But he did have Devin. He had us.

And here he was, taking care of me.

"I know you hate this, baby."

"I'm sorry," I whispered.

"Don't be sorry. You're allowed to get drunk. If your

door and blinds had been closed, you would have been safe."

"How stupid. I'm so stupid."

"No, you're not. You're allowed to make bad decisions. You weren't driving, you weren't doing anything to others. So, it's all good. And you know one of your brothers could have been here at any moment if you needed them. And the girls just left you alone. And I'm here now. We're all here for you. Okay?"

I shook my head and leaned into him, sighing.

"I'm drunk. I'm in a bathroom. And I'm pretty much naked."

"I noticed."

"I would punch you, but I don't have the energy."

"Tequila does that."

"I hate this," I repeated.

"I know, baby. Okay, let's get some water and aspirin into you, and then I'm going to tuck you into bed."

"I shouldn't."

"You shouldn't go to bed?"

"I shouldn't have done this. Shouldn't have done any of this. I should have kept things the way they were."

"You're mumbling again, but I think I got that. That fucking asshole shouldn't have led you on. But I don't want to get into that. Let's get you into bed," he whispered, his lips at my temple. He helped me brush my teeth, something I was very grateful for even in my drunken state, and then walked me to the bedroom.

I peeled away from him, taking off my shirt as I did. I could have sworn I heard a groan come out of Tucker's mouth, but I ignored it.

That's when I remembered that I wasn't wearing a bra.

But my back was to him. That was fine. Hopefully, I wouldn't remember this in the morning.

I went to my dresser, found another shirt, and pulled it over my head. Then I caught my reflection in the mirror. And not only *mine*. That's when I realized that Tucker had closed his eyes, probably because my boobs were on full display in the mirror—hard nipples and all.

Oh, good. I'd just shown Tucker more of myself than I had with Tobey.

I was on a roll.

I tried to turn on my heel to get into bed and almost fell. Thankfully, Tucker was there. He picked me up again.

He was so hard, so warm.

I closed my eyes and mumbled something, not even sure what I said.

I could feel the soft cotton of the sheets beneath my hands as he slid me into bed, but then I sneezed. Somehow that made everything worse. I smashed my forehead into his, and he cursed, falling into bed with me.

It might have been funny, but I was too tired to think about it or care. Instead, I rolled over on the very hard yet warm surface beneath me and promptly fell asleep.

# FOUR

*Tucker*

I woke up nestled against soft curves with my raging erection pressed along plump and luscious ass cheeks.

Fuck.

I knew I should have peeled Amelia off me after we'd fallen into bed, but I hadn't been able to. She'd been so warm and soft, and my brain had hurt like a motherfucker after she'd knocked her head against mine.

Last night had been a set of complications, one after another. After I'd stop laughing with her passed out on my chest, I'd tried to get her off me so I could leave.

Only the woman clung in her drunken sleep, and I couldn't bear to move her.

When she moaned and slid into deeper unconsciousness, I simply sighed and went to sleep right next to her.

Probably not the best idea, but I hadn't been able to help it.

It was hard to make good choices when it came to her, apparently.

But that wasn't something I wanted to think about.

I let my hand stroke down her hip, and I knew it had to be an unconscious thing. I was totally not doing this on my own. Because if I were, that made me evil. A lecher.

When my hand slid up to her waist, I paused, holding back a groan.

It was really hard to stop, but I did. I resisted. See? I wasn't that much of a lecher.

I pulled away and tried to move my groin from her posterior area. Only, when I did, she nestled back, pressing more firmly into my already too-hard cock.

Of course.

Apparently, this was how today was going to go.

I mean, why wouldn't this get even more awkward?

I sighed and lay there, hoping she would wake up so we could forget this ever happened. Because we really needed to forget this ever happened.

This wasn't the first time I had woken up in a woman's bed. Though I tried not to do it often. Usually, I left the night of or at least before we started spooning like Amelia and I were right now.

But I didn't think I'd ever slept in the same bed as a woman before, not without actually doing something beforehand, and not for the whole night.

Well, well, tonight was certainly one of firsts.

The first time I saw Amelia naked—at least mostly. The first time I saw her that drunk.

The first time I held her hair back as she threw up.

The first time I brushed a woman's teeth.

First time I slept in the same bed as a woman without having any type of sex.

Oh, yeah, did I mention it was the first time I saw Amelia naked?

I really needed to make sure that was out there, and that everybody knew. Because I saw Amelia Carr almost naked.

I had a feeling that she hadn't actually meant to do that.

But I kept seeing those perfect breasts of hers, such perfect tits.

Perfect nipples.

She hadn't known that her reflection was in the mirror like that. At least not at first. And I hadn't said anything.

And I was probably going to hell for that. Sure, I had closed my eyes, but not quickly enough. Because I had seen those tits. They were firm, high, and tight. With perfect pink nipples.

They were hard, pebbled. Either she was cold or

aroused. Or maybe just drunk. I didn't know at the time, but I hadn't looked too hard. At least, I tried not to.

But I liked nipples. I enjoyed all colors of them. Dark, light, brown, tan, pink, red. I adored all variations.

I was a tit man. I couldn't help it. Yeah, I was also an ass man. And the more I thought about Amelia's curves, the more I knew I was going to hell.

I couldn't stop thinking about those tits, those perfect breasts. Big enough to overfill my hand, but I'd be able to squeeze and mold them as I slid my cock between them, fucking her breasts as I came all over her chest.

God, I had to stop thinking about things like that.

Because the more I did, the more likely it would be that I would thrust against her, slowly rocking into her ass, then slide between those cheeks and into that wet heat of hers.

No, I had to stop.

I held back a groan and tried to think of gross things. Baseball. Baseball could calm me. I didn't like baseball.

What about my grandma? No, that wouldn't work. I hadn't really met her. I'd think of someone else's grandma, but that wasn't going to help either.

Ball sacks. Yeah, I could think about ball sacks. Those were kind of gross. I liked my own well enough, but they were all wrinkly and weird.

Yes, ball sacks.

Of course, now I was thinking about ball sacks and my

dick, and the fact that it was hard and pressed against her ass, and all I wanted to do was slide inside.

Not even inside her wet heat, but her ass, because I wanted to fuck that, too.

I really needed to stop.

Why hadn't I noticed her body before? I had. I must have.

But why didn't I know these curves existed?

She had that hourglass shape that begged for a man's hands. For *my* hands. And my mouth.

No, I couldn't go there. But I totally wanted to.

Of course, then there was the whole idea of doing naughty things to her as she did equally wicked things to me. But that wasn't going to happen. It couldn't.

I hadn't really noticed her curves before because I shouldn't have. And she was usually dressed in work clothes, and more often than not, covered in dirt. I liked her covered in dirt. It meant that she worked with her hands, and I knew she was damn good at her job.

In dirt. Dirty. Filthy.

Wrong direction for my thoughts.

I had seen her in a bathing suit before so I knew she had curves, but I hadn't noticed them. No, I had told myself *not* to notice them.

Because if I noticed them, then I'd want them.

I would want *her.*

And I couldn't. She was my best friend's little sister.

Devin would not only kill me, he'd also probably castrate and do other horrific things to me.

Not because he was an overprotective asshole, but because he knew me. I was good with women, great with them actually. I was kind, but I wasn't in the market for a commitment. I knew what happened when you fell in love with someone too hard and too fast. You ended up getting married and having babies when you shouldn't. You ended up doing stupid shit that got you killed and then sent your kid off to multiple foster homes.

And then that kid, with asthma and night terrors of the times his parents were always drunk and high ended up in foster care until he was eighteen. Because nobody really wanted a kid with guaranteed high medical bills and night terrors.

Yeah, that's what happened when you stuck with one woman when you weren't that type of person.

I never cheated, never dated more than one woman at a time, but I did not need anything else.

I was fine the way I was.

And if I kept telling myself that, then maybe I would believe it.

But it wasn't like Devin's parents were any better.

Devin's mom had cheated more than once, I remembered that much from Devin's drunken rants when we were in college and getting drunk on cheap beer and grain alcohol.

The Carrs' dad had drunk himself to death, so we didn't really get drunk all that often. We still didn't. But there had been that one time with the grain alcohol. Never again.

I held back a shudder, even as my hands tightened on Amelia's waist.

I really needed to get out of this bed.

It was just...the moment I did that, she would wake up, and everything would change.

No, it wouldn't. I wouldn't let it.

Everything would be fine.

Before I could think about anything more, though, she let out a groan. I froze.

My hand was still on her waist, my cock still pressed against her butt. Maybe she wouldn't notice. Perhaps she would think it was morning wood. Maybe I should, too. Yes, it was totally that. It wasn't the inappropriate thoughts currently running rampant through my brain.

"Tobey?" she asked, her voice sounding like sandpaper.

Well. That put me in my place, didn't it? Made sense, though. Didn't it? Of course, it would be Tobey behind her with his cock pressed against her. Totally not me. Amelia and I weren't even great friends. I was better friends with Devin. Amelia was just there. Like I was.

I cleared my throat and slowly pulled my softening erection from her backside. Listening to the woman you were currently thinking dirty thoughts about saying another man's name really wasn't a turn-on.

And, yeah, I was an asshole. But I had earned that title.

"Not Tobey," I said, trying to sound cheery and wide-awake. I was fine. Everything was fine.

"Tucker?" she asked, frozen against me.

"Yep. You fell asleep on top of me, and then I passed out. Sorry about that." I quickly rolled out of bed, tapped her side as I did, and rose up on my feet. I was still dressed, even in my shoes, and figured everything was fine. She would get over this, like I would, and we wouldn't talk about it again. And we would definitely not tell Devin. Hopefully, he hadn't driven by at any point because my car was in front of her house. Dear God. Wouldn't that be an interesting conversation if it happened?

"Oh my God." She sat up, her tank top askew so one breast was exposed, peeking its little nipple at me.

Oh God, why was she making this so difficult?

I closed my eyes and gestured with my hand at her chest after I'd cleared my throat.

"You better uh, fix yourself."

She looked down, or at least I think she did, I didn't really know since my eyes were closed and I was so not peeking. And then she laughed. "Well, that's just fine, isn't it?" I heard her rustling the sheets, and then she laughed. "You can open your eyes now."

She was standing in her tank top, perfectly covered up, and now in shorts. I didn't know where she had found them, but at least she was fully dressed.

"So, yeah," she said softly. Then she looked at my face, her eyes wide. "You have a red spot on your forehead. Did I do that?" She rubbed her own head and winced.

"Yep. You hit me really hard with your head as you sneezed. That's how we both ended up like we did. But I'm fine. And you're going to be okay. Right?"

"I think so." She looked so lost, I felt bad. So, I walked around the bed and opened my arms for her. See? Everything would be fine. We could be casual about this.

"Come here, talk to Uncle Tucker." That wasn't creepy at all.

She looked wary but still took a few steps forward before wrapping her arms around my waist. She rested her head on my chest and let out a sigh. I hugged her, but not too tightly. Nothing weird. I didn't want her to feel uncomfortable. And I sure as hell didn't want to feel any more uncomfortable than I already did.

"I'm sorry." She whispered the words, and I didn't know what she was apologizing for. Probably a little bit of everything—and nothing.

"You have nothing to be sorry for." I put my hands on her shoulders and pushed her away so I could look at her face. "Things happen. You feel any better?"

"I have a headache."

"Well, that was a lot of tequila. You tossed most of it, and I gave you some aspirin, but you're going to feel a little bad today. But that's fine. You're allowed to be a little bad once in a while."

"I'm sorry you had to take care of me."

"It's what I do, Amelia. We're family." I smiled as I said it, knowing that I'd just had very non-family-type thoughts about her earlier. But I wasn't going to think about it. Because if I did, things would only get weirder.

"If you say so. But I don't think I'm ever going to be able to face you again."

"You're facing me right now." I leaned down and smacked a kiss on her lips. Then grinned. "Now, go take a shower and get to work. You have things to do today, young lady. And so do I. You're going to be fine. You don't need to think about that asshole ever again."

"Everyone keeps calling him names."

"Well, we love you. It's what we do. Now, chop-chop. Get to work." I pushed her towards the shower and then headed out of her bedroom without a backward glance. Because if I looked, I was going to think of her in the shower. And I really shouldn't do that.

I quickly cleaned up a little bit of the tequila mess from the night before since she didn't follow me, and then I headed to my car, knowing that I needed to rush if I was going to make it to work on time. People relied on me, and I needed to make sure I deserved that trust. After all, I was a radiologist, and I worked my ass off. I probably shouldn't show up smelling like vomit and tequila or whatever else had stuck to me from last night.

But I knew better. I didn't smell like any of those. I smelled like her. And that was even worse.

Hopefully, she would be okay. But even if she wasn't, she had others to take care of her.

I didn't need to be that person.

Thankfully, I didn't live too far away, hence why I'd told myself it was okay to go and check on her last night.

In retrospect, it *had* been a good idea because I had helped her. But I still didn't know why I had gone in the first place. Maybe because everybody had seemed so worried about her. And I had seen that pity. I hated pity. As a foster kid, I'd gotten enough pity throughout my life. And everyone had looked at Amelia with a similar pity the other night. And I hadn't liked it.

So, I wanted to be there for her, to check on her. Not to look down on her in any way. Because there was nothing superior about me. I only wanted to make sure that she was moving on and finding what she needed. Even if I didn't know if that was my place.

Sleeping in her bed while pressed up against her hadn't been in the plans, of course, but I wasn't going to look a gift horse in the mouth. Not that it was a gift. It couldn't be.

Of course, as I got into the shower, my cock had a different idea.

Everything was fine. I wasn't going to think too hard about it. I would just go with the flow.

It was okay to do this once.

I quickly soaped myself up and grabbed the base of my cock, giving it a squeeze before sliding up and down my length.

I imagined Amelia in with me, those firm tits of hers wrapped around my cock as I slowly slid between them, the tip resting against her plump lips as I did.

I'd thrust slowly, one, two, three times. And then her lips would part, and her tongue would dash out, licking the seam.

I had to hold myself back at merely the thought of that warm mouth enveloping me.

And then she'd open her mouth more, and I'd slide my cock between those two tits a little harder, right into that open, accepting mouth.

She'd hum along my length, swallowing me deep down into her throat. I'd be too big for her, so she'd have to wrap her hands around the base, squeezing me as she bobbed her head. But then I would take control. I'd wrap her long hair around my hand and tug. She'd wince at the slight pain, but then she would get wet because of it. She'd moan, opening her jaw a bit more so I could properly fuck her mouth, sliding down her throat as she took more of me. Wanted more. She'd dig her fingernails into my thighs and my ass, begging for more of my cock.

And just as I was about to come, I'd pull out completely, bend down, pick her up by the thighs, and slam her onto my cock—one quick thrust that would send us both into orgasm.

And then I'd keep her on me, set her on the ledge I built into my shower, and I'd pump in and out of her, hard and fast until we both came, the water going cold around me.

Simply the idea of it, of her lips on mine, on my cock, of us touching, had me coming, my balls tightening as I spurted all over the shower wall. The water grew cold around me, like in my fantasy, and I quickly washed up, cleaning the wall as I did.

I hadn't come that hard by myself in a while, and it was a little disconcerting. But that was fine. Everything was okay.

I finished my shower and dried off, knowing that I had to hurry if I was going to make it to work on time. I looked down at my phone, hoping that Amelia had texted saying that she was okay or something. Not that I wanted Amelia to text me. She wasn't going to text me. Why would she?

Instead, I saw that I had a missed call from someone. Someone from my past that I hadn't seen in a while.

Interesting. I hadn't seen Melinda in a few years, and I wondered what she wanted.

I knew she had moved to the other side of the city a while ago, and we had called it quits after a few nights together. It hadn't been serious, but it had been fun.

She hadn't been for me, and I sure as hell hadn't been right for her.

I shrugged since she hadn't left a message. I figured she would probably text if she really wanted something.

No need to worry. I had other things on my mind. And the main one had to be work. Something I loved.

It couldn't be Amelia. It really couldn't and shouldn't be Amelia Carr.

# FIVE

*Amelia*

ON A LIST OF THE TOP TEN MOST EMBARRASSING events of the past week, I wasn't sure where I'd rank the thing with Tucker versus the one with Tobey. Both were at least a seventy, but which was worse?

Showing the goods and professing my love for my best friend only to find out that he didn't love me at all?

Or getting so drunk that I nearly puked on my brother's best friend before getting naked in front of him by accident and then practically sleeping on him for the whole night before calling him by another man's name?

Which was worse?

There really wasn't an answer.

Because they were both horrible. And I didn't want to face any of it.

So, I'd work.

And plan.

And do anything that wasn't thinking about my poor life choices.

What I really wanted to do today was go out, get sweaty, and work. I wanted to be covered in dirt and just get shit done. Only we were nearing the holidays. And I lived in Denver fucking Colorado. That meant there was snow on the ground. And the earth was hard as ice. That was fine, I still had plenty to do considering that I'd added a greenhouse and other buildings onto my property. The frost wasn't going to kick my ass.

But, unfortunately, I couldn't go outside and let the sun beat down on my face. Because while the sun was out, it was frigid outside. So cold, my bones ached at the thought of it. I wasn't even old enough to have aching bones, but here I was, hurting. Because of the cold. It was fine. Mostly because I needed it to be fine. I needed everything to be okay.

I might not be able to work outside, but I could work in my greenhouse. And get sweaty. And do all those normal things that usually calmed me. At least, I could try.

So, I put on my work boots, tried to ignore the pounding in my head, and headed out to my truck.

I had a few clients who needed some things done.

Mostly maintenance on stuff they hadn't winterized in time. While those clients used to be on contract, some of them had decided to terminate their contracts to see if they could do things on their own. And while I did my best to make sure everybody knew what they needed to do to keep plants alive, some people thought they had black thumbs, and then they proved to themselves that they had those black thumbs. I would help them get things fixed, and that was fine. I would teach them again, or I would just put them back under contract. Plants were life. They were literal life. Sometimes, things didn't work out the way you wanted, and you needed a gentle helping hand. Or maybe even a firm one. I would figure it out, it's what I did. And if I focused on work and what I needed to do there, I wouldn't stress out about everything else as much.

Or, at least that's what I told myself.

Because I really didn't want to think about Tobey. Or Tucker. Apparently, it was my curse to make a fool of myself in front of men having names starting with *T*.

I was such an idiot.

No, I needed to stop degrading myself. People made mistakes. Then they got over them. I would get over this.

Eventually. Maybe no more tequila, though. Ever.

Yes, that was a saying that people used when they didn't really mean it. But I was not going to drink tequila, ever again. At least not in those copious amounts. Because...dear God.

"Time to get going," I told myself as I pulled into my place. I'd spent a good chunk of change as well as some of the bank's to afford this little piece of paradise, but it was worth it.

I had my main building where people could come in for meetings and where I displayed a small showcase of what I could do. But my pride and joy was my greenhouse and the growing areas. Even though it was winter, I had things to do, and dirt to play with. Once I got dirty and had a little soil under my fingernails, I knew I'd be able to breathe again. I'd be able to bury all of the crap that had happened recently and just *be*.

At least, I hoped so.

Amelia's Greens was technically closed for the day, and I didn't have any appointments unless something came up later. That meant I could put in my earbuds and simply *work*.

The heat slid along my skin as I walked into my greenhouse. The familiar scents of plants, potting soil, flowers, greens, and pottery filled my nose, and I smiled.

This was home.

This would make everything okay.

And if it didn't?

Well, I sure as hell wouldn't be drinking tequila to try and fix things.

I let myself fall into my work for a good hour before I paused to take a drink and check my email. It was just the normal things. If I tried hard enough, I could imagine that I wasn't here trying to ignore the rest of the world. But that I was getting work done and doing something I loved.

But every time I paused, each time I let my mind drift, I imagined the look on Tobey's face, and then I imagined what Tucker had probably looked like when he saw me in my drunken state.

I owed him.

Not Tobey. I didn't know what to think about him. But I really owed Tucker. I had acted like a fool, and while I had been in my own home, I hadn't really been safe, and he'd been there to take care of me.

Maybe I should do something for him. Like, bake him a pie or something. I could bake, not as good as Erin could, but that was her job.

When I got home, I would bake him something. In fact, I was almost done for the day, so I would head to the grocery store, pick up what I needed, and then bake.

That would make things right. And once that was over, I would only have to worry about Tobey. Not that I had any idea what to do about that.

I went back to work for a bit more, and then cleaned up and made a quick mental checklist of what I'd need from the store.

I didn't bake often, but I had at least some of the staples. I'd need to get a lot of the things that went inside a pie, though.

Thankfully, I had a change of clothes in my truck, so I quickly washed up in my office bathroom—complete with a shower and a tub—then put my hair in a braid, stuffed a hat on my head so I didn't catch a cold since it was still freezing outside, and then headed to the grocery store.

My phone buzzed as I was heading down the produce aisle, figuring out if I wanted to make a cherry or an apple pie. Would a cherry apple pie work? I didn't have a recipe for that, but I figured I could find one really quick.

I looked down at the screen and tried not to wince.

**Erin:** *We're heading over soon. We heard Tucker was over?*

**Zoey:** *Yes, Tucker mentioned to Devin who told Erin that he came over after we left. What happened?*

Oh good. Tucker couldn't keep his damn mouth shut. Great.

**Me:** *I'm at the grocery store. Be home in a bit.*

I didn't explain, but I knew I would have to when I saw them.

**Erin:** *You better explain.*

Yeah, I'd have to. But explain what? The fact that I was an idiot? That I made poor decisions?

I was pretty sure they already knew that.

A little deflated because I would soon have to relive the previous night, I quickly decided to go with an apple pie instead of looking up a new recipe, and then went to check out.

Traffic was easy on my way home, so I beat Erin and Zoey to my place and started working on the pie.

I decided to go with a pre-made crust, mostly because I didn't have a lot of time. I hoped he wouldn't notice or care. It wasn't really baking, but it would have to do.

Maybe I'd actually make a real pie for him some other time.

Before I could lament more about going with a pre-made crust considering that it wasn't really baking, the doorbell rang. I sighed.

Time to step up.

Zoey and Erin were at the door as if they'd already been together, and I narrowed my eyes.

"So, is the inquisition going to begin, then?" I asked, a little snap to my voice.

Erin's eyes widened, and Zoey took a step back.

Okay, I guess there was a little bit more than just a *little* bite to my tone.

"What do you mean, an inquisition?" Zoey asked, her voice timid.

"We were worried about you."

"Come on in. It's cold out. And you don't need to worry about me. I'm fine."

I took a step back, and the others came in. I tried to calm my insides. I didn't want to sound rude, or like a bitch. But I was tired. And it felt like I kept making mistakes. I didn't want to relive it with my friends.

Except they were my friends. I should be able to tell them anything. Right?

"Apparently, after you left, I didn't close the door all the way. When Tucker drove by—I'm still not sure why—he saw the door open and came in. And I drank a little too much tequila after you left."

"You were drinking wine when we left. Not even a lot of it. You went to tequila?" Erin asked. And there it was again. The pity. I hated the pity.

"Well, I had a bad day. I felt like tequila was what I needed. Not that I'm ever going to do it again."

"And did anything happen?" Erin asked, a little hope in her voice. Well, that wasn't good. There was nothing between Tucker and me. Something I was very sure about, and something I hoped they'd be sure about soon, too.

"No. He just took care of me. I still can't believe Tucker told my brother." I grumbled the last bit as I slid the pie into the oven, but I didn't miss the look shared between my friends.

"Well, I was in the other room when he was talking to Devin. He had to drop something off or something. I'm not sure. Anyway, I don't think he meant to tell him. More like Devin asked what Tucker did last night, and he mentioned seeing you. It didn't sound weird or anything. But I don't think anyone wants to hide anything, you know? We're all friends. We take care of each other."

"I know we do. I was just surprised."

I was not going to mention the whole naked thing, or the fact that he'd slept over. Because by the sound of it, Tucker hadn't mentioned that, and I wasn't going to be the one that opened that bag of kittens.

"I'm fine. Tucker made sure I didn't swallow my tongue or anything. And he took the tequila away."

"Like a good friend," Zoey said. "You know what I mean, a friend hands you the tequila, and then makes sure you don't go overboard with it. You should have told us you were going to start drinking the hard stuff. We could've stayed."

"Totally. In fact, it was because I went out drinking and had tequila that I met Devin again," Erin put in. "It's sort of my drink."

I smiled and shook my head, cleaning up around the kitchen as the girls helped me. They didn't even have to ask, they just jumped right in, helping me put things away. I grinned. I would do the same for them. It was nice that they felt comfortable enough in my home to do that.

Zoey had been my friend for a while, but we had gotten closer over the past few months. I only knew Erin in passing when we were growing up, but now that she was with my brother, we were close.

I also spent a lot of time with my sister-in-law, Thea, but since she was an hour away, I didn't see her as much as I would like.

I should drive down soon and go see them. And, of

course, get some cake at Thea's bakery. The fact that I had two bakers in my family now was quite a treat. And though I was the one baking a pie today, and especially considering that it was practically store-bought, it wouldn't be as good as theirs. But it was fine. I wasn't going to eat this one anyway. Even if just the thought of it made me want to go back on the elliptical so I could try a slice.

"So, have you heard from Tobey?" Zoey asked, a little cautious.

I held back a wince, even if it felt as if someone were scraping out my heart.

But I would be fine. We would be friends again. We needed to talk.

Eventually.

"No. But it's okay."

I think we all knew that was a lie, but nobody was going to say it. It was going to be all right.

"Maybe he needs to see you going out on dates," Erin said. "I know it won't be easy, but when you're ready, maybe going out and having some fun and just being with someone will not only help you but also help him see that you're over him or whatever."

"Yeah, that's a great idea. I'm sure between Erin and I, we could find someone for you."

I knew that they were trying to help. But the fact that I didn't know how anyone could help meant that it hurt. I didn't know what to say, and I didn't know what to do.

But I would figure it out. I had to.

Though merely the idea of dating someone other than Tobey hurt. I needed to talk to him. I needed it to be okay.

But I didn't know how to do that.

I didn't think there was any way *to* do that.

"Maybe," I said, knowing it didn't really sound like I meant it.

But they let me be, and we talked about nothing. Just pie and the fact that I was bringing it to Tucker later as a thank you. Oh, and tequila. We talked about that, too.

These were my friends, people I could count on. And I would be able to rely on Tobey again, too.

I had to believe that.

The girls left, and I had a feeling that they were going to try setting me up on dates soon if I wasn't careful. I wasn't ready for that. But they wanted to help, so they were latching on to the one thing they could do.

I set the pie to cool and went to let my hair out of its braid, the waves falling around my face.

I quickly put on some makeup and changed my shirt.

I wasn't getting ready for Tucker necessarily, but the fact that I'd been a complete mess and half-naked the last time he saw me told me that I needed to step it up a bit. I wasn't trying to look good for him. Not in the slightest. Just trying to look good for myself.

To prove to myself and him that I wasn't a complete dork.

I quickly put the pie in a carrier, one that I had gotten for Christmas one year and was thankful I had stored away in a cupboard, and headed over to Tucker's.

I hadn't called or texted to see if he was even there. Hopefully, I wouldn't have to leave it on his porch where it could freeze.

Apparently, I wasn't really firing on all cylinders right now.

I parked in Tucker's driveway, though I still didn't know if he was home. He parked in the garage, so I couldn't tell if his vehicle was here. Then I grabbed the pie and got out of my truck, hoping he was home. It was cold as I walked up, and that's when I realized that I really had no idea what I was going to say.

*Thanks for not commenting on my boobs.*

Oh, yeah, that's what I should lead with.

I rang the doorbell and waited for a bit, long enough that I was afraid he wasn't home.

Great. This wasn't going to be awkward at all. Leaving a pie on the doorstep, then having to text that I had done so.

*Thanks for taking away the tequila, here's pie.*

Cold pie that's probably ruined and practically store-bought.

Dear God, I was a mess.

No wonder Tobey didn't want me.

And that was enough of that. No more pity parties. He was my friend. I just wasn't going to be in love with him anymore. And I was going to thank Tucker for helping me out in a bad situation. Everything would go back to normal.

The door opened, and my eyes went to a very wet, very naked chest.

Dear God and everything that's holy and sweaty and delicious.

I had slept against that chest all night, yet I still couldn't believe what I was seeing.

It was all hard lines and plains, and every inch of him was slick and ready for teeth.

It looked as if he had just gotten out of the shower, his hair falling over his face before he used his arm to slick it back. I couldn't help but follow the long lines of his biceps as they bulged when he did so.

I swallowed hard, avoiding his face, my gaze sliding down his body, across his muscled chest, down his eight-pack—not even a six, an eight—and then along the long lines of his torso.

He had those V lines, the ones that some called the Adonis lines. I called them lickable, biteable ones.

Oh, yes, they were the come-to-Mama lines.

I was going to hell.

But I couldn't help but look at those grooves, or the neat trail of hair that led to where his towel rested very low on his hips.

So low, in fact, I caught a sexy glimpse of thigh at the gap in his towel.

It wasn't even secured, except for his fingers grabbing it tightly in a fist.

Dear, God.

I'd known my brother's best friend was hot, but I didn't realize he was *this* hot.

He was like all the good Chrises rolled up into one Avenger. And naked.

Yep, I was going to hell.

"You okay there, Amelia?"

My eyes shot up to his face, and I saw the laughter there.

"I baked you a pie," I said and shoved it at him.

He used his free hand to grab it from me. Thankfully, he didn't release the towel.

That would have been awkward.

But again, I had gotten mostly naked in front of him already. It should be his turn.

No, there would be no turns.

This was bad. This was so, *so* bad.

"You baked me a pie?"

I nodded quickly. "Yes. And...thanks for the tequila. I mean, thanks for taking care of me after the tequila. Anyway, it's cold, and your nipples are hard."

I snapped my lips shut, and he threw back his head and laughed.

"Yeah, it is cold enough that my nipples are hard. Thanks for noticing. Do you want to come in?"

"I really don't."

I really did. No, I did not.

"Okay, thanks for the pie. You didn't have to do that."

"Yeah, I did. So, I'm going to go home now. But thanks again. Seriously. I don't know what I would have done without you."

"I'll always try to be there for you." His eyes went somber, and his smile was a little soft. "You're practically family, Amelia. Of course, I'll be there."

I ignored the little clutch I felt at the word *family* because it really didn't matter. He *was* family. He was practically my brother's brother. And there were rules about that.

Even though I would likely have some really dirty thoughts about him later. I couldn't help it. He was in a towel.

"Well, I should go. Good luck with your towel."

Sheer mortification rolled through me again, and I ran toward my truck.

His laughter followed me, and I resisted the urge to flip him off. I was going to hell, but it would be fun on the way.

I was doing my best to force out the visions of what lay under that towel as I pulled into my driveway—and almost slammed into the garage door.

Someone was on my porch. Someone I wanted to see with every fiber of my being, though someone I knew I couldn't see.

I turned off my truck and slowly got out, trying to calm

my heartbeat. Attempting to swallow the bile in the back of my throat.

Why was my mouth so dry? And why were my hands so damp?

Tobey stood up and slid his hands into his pants' pockets.

His hair flopped over his face, but he didn't move it back. It took everything within me not to race over there and do it for him.

I used to have that right. At least I *thought* I had.

Now, I had clearly crossed a line, and I didn't know if I could ever come back from that.

"You're here," I said, surprising myself.

"We need to talk," he said. I nodded.

"Yeah, we do. And I need to apologize. Why don't we go inside?"

"We need to talk right now, okay?"

I nodded tightly, drawing in my stomach. "Okay."

"You're still my friend, Amelia."

"That's good because I always want to be. You're my friend, too, Tobey."

"You're always going to be my friend."

There was an episode of *The Big Bang Theory* when someone said that the word *always* didn't sound good every time. This was one of those times. *Always* made it worse.

"Let's just forget about everything. Let's start from where we were before all of this happened."

I didn't miss the wince that flashed across his face, and my heart shattered a bit more. A little clink sounded as a piece fell off, metal on a tile floor as it echoed throughout the cavernous hole of my soul.

"I need some time." He swallowed hard, and I looked directly into his eyes, hoping that he wasn't about to break the rest of me. But I had to remember, this was my fault. This was all my fault. "Beth needs some time, too."

*Beth.* Okay.

"You told her."

"She's my everything, Amelia. I told you that. I had to tell her."

"I thought I was your everything."

I hadn't meant to say the words, and my eyes widened as I did. He simply looked at me, that same pitying expression I'd been getting a lot lately on his face. I hated it.

"You know what? Forget I said that. Time. We can do time."

"It might be a lot of time. Beth? She means everything to me. And it's just different now with you."

I smiled and kept nodding. I couldn't say anything. What was so different?

Yes, I had professed something to him, but he hadn't told me about her. Why hadn't he said anything? I could have saved us a lot of pain.

If she was his everything and I wasn't, why hadn't he mentioned her to me? To anyone?

And why did it hurt so much that he hadn't?

He kept looking at me, and then he walked away. He didn't touch me, didn't say a word. He didn't even say goodbye.

Why did that hurt so much?

And why did I feel as if I had just lost my best friend?

I slowly walked into the house, closed the door behind me, and then sat on the floor, my back against the wood.

The tears fell, and I hated myself. Because I didn't want to cry anymore. I didn't want to feel that pity, especially for myself.

But I didn't know how else to feel.

Because I had thought I loved my best friend. But what if I was wrong? What if I didn't know anything?

# Six

*Tucker*

Out of all the reasons I was going to hell, one of them was undoubtedly the fact that I couldn't stop waking up in the mornings with my hand around my cock in response to very sexy dreams involving the sweet sister of a friend that I shouldn't even be thinking about.

I wasn't a teenager anymore, but apparently, that's what my dick did. I thought of Amelia in my sleep, had various dreams of us fucking on different pieces of furniture around my house and hers, then woke up either needing to come or already coming in my sheets.

I'd given up sleeping in pajamas at this point, it only added laundry. But that meant I had to wash my sheets, over and over again.

It was exhausting, and I had to work.

I also had to face Devin every time I saw him and hope like hell that he didn't know that I was thinking dirty thoughts about his sister. That I was doing wicked things to her every night in my mind.

What the hell was wrong with me? Sure, I loved women. I'd been with my fair share of them. I wasn't a complete manwhore, but my number wasn't that small either.

I was safe, clean, and liked having sex.

I could probably go out and find a date if I needed one. Maybe I should. Perhaps it'd get my mind off Amelia.

But that was really fucking hard to do when all I did was think of her, even when I shouldn't.

I needed to get over this by being the man I should be.

By being her friend.

Because thinking about her any other way would likely get my dick ripped off by her big brother. Maybe even by Amelia herself.

Because, yeah, she liked the way I looked. I could tell. It was hard not to notice when she kept looking at me the way she did when I was in that towel. It was really difficult not to get hard in front of her.

If she'd kept looking at me like that, I wouldn't have been able to hide my erection.

As it was, I'd held pretty tightly to my control, trying not to lose it.

But she'd looked, practically smacking her lips together and licking them.

Much as I'd done when she took off her shirt in front of me.

The difference was, she had been drunk and hadn't really known what she was doing.

I was not an asshole. Okay, I was, but I wasn't a sadistic pervert or anything.

That meant I needed to be Amelia's friend. And that was why I was in the grocery store, picking up a few things for her house.

Devin had mentioned the other night that she had been working hard on a couple of projects, throwing herself into her work rather than actually talking about Tobey or dealing with what had happened there.

I was glad that she wasn't talking about the asshole because I wanted to kick Tobey's little ass.

What the hell was wrong with him? Sure, maybe he hadn't known that Amelia had feelings for him, but he'd hidden a girlfriend. If you were going to start hiding shit like that, there were reasons. Things that made Tobey not good enough for Amelia.

So, I was going to make sure she was okay. I had the night off and needed to eat dinner, so I was going to force her to eat my cooking.

We were friends, and we'd basically seen each other

naked at this point. We'd slept in the same bed. I figured we'd passed the line into a new kind of friendship.

One where I could make her eat my cooking, and hope she didn't look as exhausted as she had the last time I saw her.

I really wanted to kick Tobey's ass.

I ignored the come-on from the lady in the pasta department, and the one from the man in the meat section—because that wasn't a cliché or anything. Apparently, this time of the evening was when all the singles went out in my town to try and find a date. I'd have to think about that the next time I went out. Maybe I could find a date. And it would not be with Amelia. We were friends. Damn it.

I needed to stop having dreams about her. Fantasies about her and those very hot nipples. Ones that begged for my mouth.

Just as I imagined her mouth on my body as she had moved the towel away from me before going down to her knees. And that was enough of that.

I really did not need a hard-on as I drove toward Amelia's house.

I pulled up into her driveway and went to get my groceries from the back.

Thankfully, I only had three big bags. Of course, they were the reusable bags that held a lot more stuff than the plastic ones, so I might've gone a little overboard. But Amelia needed groceries.

Or maybe Devin was simply being overprotective. After all, that's what big brothers did.

I rang the doorbell and figured that I was either making a colossal mistake, or I was doing the right thing.

I wanted to do the right thing.

Amelia opened the door, and I held back a wince.

Her hair was a little greasy, piled up on the top of her head. She had dark circles under her eyes, and I swore she had lost at least ten pounds over the past couple of weeks.

She had on baggy sweats, a tank with no bra—damn her and those nipples!—and a zippered sweatshirt that she hadn't zipped up. She wore no shoes, no makeup, and even though she still looked beautiful, she looked exhausted. And sad.

I wanted to hold her close and tell her that everything would be okay.

But because I couldn't really do that, I was going to at least try to cook for her.

"Tucker?"

I grinned and pushed past her. I probably should've waited for an invitation, but I was afraid that she might not give me one, and I needed to take care of her. She needed to eat.

"I'm cooking you dinner."

"Excuse me?"

I just grinned and acted like this was totally normal. It wasn't normal at all.

I set the bags on the counter and smiled. "I'm cooking you dinner."

"Why?"

"Because you need it. You need food. I need food. So, I'm making it."

She folded her arms under her breasts, and it made the silken white skin of her mounds peek out from her tank a bit more.

Damn it. This was not going to help my dreams later.

"Because you feel bad for me, too?"

"No."

That was the truth. I didn't feel bad for her. I was angry, but there wasn't any pity there. I didn't feel bad at all.

She needed someone, and I was it.

"I don't really believe you."

"You don't have to. But you're going to eat my fucking cooking."

"Well, that sounds nice."

"I'm an amazing cook. Ask any of the women I've dated." I winked, and she just rolled her eyes. But I saw humor there. Sometimes, a little self-deprecating humor helped.

"So, you're good at breakfast?" she asked, and I shook my head.

"Dinner, honey. They never stay the night."

"You are a manwhore."

"Am not."

"Yeah, that's not what Devin says. Caleb, too. I think even Dimitri's mentioned it."

"Your brothers have a very low opinion of me, apparently."

"My brothers love you."

I let that settle into me and smiled. They were my family. And it was nice. I was going to make sure that Amelia knew she was loved, too. Even if I wasn't really sure how to go about it. "Well, it doesn't matter if my food is good or not, you're going to eat it. However, I'm making pasta with clams and a nice wine sauce."

"Oh, that sounds amazing. I never really eat clams or anything because Dimitri's allergic."

"Yeah, shellfish allergies are not something you want to take lightly. But I remember Devin mentioning that you weren't allergic, so I figured this was fine."

"I love clams. But you really don't have to cook for me. I'll be fine."

"I already have everything here. And while I will take no for an answer if you really don't want me here—I don't want to be pushy—I don't want you to say no."

"You're riding the line of being annoying, caring, sweet, and weird all at once. I don't really know how that happens."

"It's not really a line then. More like a square. Or a circle."

"I really sucked at geometry," she said, shaking her head.

"You're a landscape architect. How are you bad at geometry?"

"It just never made sense when it was on paper. The only thing that I really understood was the trapezoid."

I paused, taking out the veggies from the bag as she came up to my side. "What do you mean, trapezoid?"

"Well, my teacher taught me that a trapezoid was like an open box that had a lid, and there was this alien called a zoid. And in order to trap the zoid, you had to put it in the box and close the lid. But when you did, the insides folded in a bit. Hence, the trapezoid."

I looked at her, blinking, and then turned my head back and laughed.

"That's ridiculous."

"I know. But I remembered it because of that. And I know that when I have children, I will help them learn what a trapezoid is from that thing I learned so many years ago. But, no, I didn't like geometry in school, even though I love the idea of it now. At least, I think I do."

"Well, you're brilliant, just so you know." I leaned down and kissed the tip of her nose. She blushed, shaking her head.

"Yeah, not so brilliant sometimes. But thanks for coming over. I guess I should actually leave the house other than for work, but I don't usually feel like it." She shrugged and stuffed her hands into her sweater pockets.

"You don't have to leave the house if you don't want to.

It's okay to have people come to you. I know Devin's busy with Erin. I haven't really seen them often. Zoey's busy, too."

"I know," Amelia said, shrugging again. "It's kind of hard to figure out what to say to Zoey sometimes anyway."

I frowned. "What do you mean?"

"About relationships? You know, I shouldn't really talk about that. It's not my business, and I'm afraid if I do, it'll sound like gossip."

I nodded, putting that tidbit of information away for later. "I get you. But if you want to talk about it, I'm here. Now, the subjects we *can* talk about are *Avengers* movies, work, animals, plants, and cookie dough." I quickly listed off the things, and she snorted.

"That's a very odd list."

"Well, since I just came up with it off the top of my head as I was speaking to you, it's a list that works."

"I still don't know why you're doing this," she said, coming up beside me to help me wash some of the produce.

"I don't know why I'm doing it either," I said honestly, my voice a whisper.

She let out a sigh beside me and then rested her head on my upper arm. "He was my friend, Tucker. I used to do this with him all the time. And now I'm afraid I'll never be able to do it again."

I ignored the comparison. "Yeah, well, your friend was kind of a dick."

"No, he wasn't." Even though she said the words, they didn't really ring true. I didn't think she actually believed them.

"Yeah, he was a dick. But I'll be your friend now. Got it?"

"Uh, no. You can't simply declare yourself my friend. Yes, we're friends, but you can't move in to that position."

"I totally believe I did. So, you're just going to have to deal with it."

She gave me a weird look and shook her head again. "I don't understand you, Tucker."

I went to fill a pot with water and pasta, and then turned to look at her. "I don't understand me sometimes either. But it's what I do. I sort of inserted myself into Devin's life when we were younger, too, and look how that turned out."

"You did?" she asked, helping me chop tomatoes.

"Yeah. I don't even remember how it started, but he hung out with me enough at school that we became friends. When he invited me over one day, I didn't want to leave."

Amelia snorted. "You didn't want to leave our house? Do you not remember the yelling?"

I reached out and squeezed her shoulder before going back to cooking, not looking at her.

"I do. But your parents were pretty good when I was there."

"At first, because you were company. And then you

weren't company anymore, you were practically one of the kids. And that meant someone had to feed you, and Dad got all pissed off at that." Amelia just rolled her eyes. "Dimitri always made sure we were good, though. He was so much older that it never felt weird. I mean, it was worse for the rest of them, I think. I had my big brothers to take care of me."

"You have a great family. And it's only growing as the guys get married."

"I know, right? I wish things had been different with my parents, but we can't go back and fix it."

"You're preaching to the choir," I said, sautéing garlic.

"Yeah, at least I had my brothers, and my dad stayed around as long as he did, you know?"

"I do. Foster care wasn't always bad. I found some good homes when I was younger, and then had a decent one for a while. But no one really wanted a kid with asthma—medical bills and all that. Plus, I had some pretty serious and stupid night terrors when I was a kid."

"I don't remember that."

"I told Devin, but he was really good at keeping my secrets, you know?"

"My brothers are the best."

"Yeah. They are." It was something I needed to remind myself if I was going to hang out with Amelia like this.

"So, night terrors?"

I shook myself out of my reverie and smiled down at her. "Yeah. Just vivid dreams. I don't even remember what they were about. I have vivid dreams now, too, though. Like as a kid."

"Really? Are they scary?"

Probably shouldn't have mentioned those dreams. "Sometimes."

Sometimes, they weren't scary at all. I really needed to shift the conversation.

"So, do you like garlic?"

"I love garlic. Although I'm really glad that we're not dating and are only friends. Because you aren't really supposed to have garlic on dates."

I raised a brow at her. "Oh, I bet if we went on a date, I could eat all the garlic I wanted. And you'd still want to kiss me." I said it so jokingly that she rolled her eyes.

"Ego much?"

"You know it. However, eat all the garlic you want. I promise to keep my mouth off you."

"You're such a giver," she said, pushing another clove of garlic at me.

"I try."

And I was trying. I was trying really hard to stop thinking about Amelia the way I was. If we kept like we were, remained in our friendship in this new iteration, it could work out. Because Amelia needed stability. She needed friends.

And I sure as hell didn't need the complication of wanting Devin's sister.

# SEVEN

*Amelia*

HANDS SLID OVER MY HIPS, SLOWLY, methodically, before running up my sides to cup my breasts, callused thumbs flicking over my hard nipples. I arched my back, wanting more, needing more.

I spread my thighs, letting him sink between my legs, his pelvis pressed against mine even though he didn't slide all the way in.

Instead, he rested against me, slowly playing with me, leading me into temptation.

And, oh how I begged for it.

He lowered his mouth, his tongue pressing firmly against my nipple before swallowing and sucking on my breasts. He paid attention to both of them, never leaving one cold.

My body ached, and I arched for him, wanting to reach between my legs and get myself off, or grab the base of him and lead him to my center. I wanted him inside me.

I needed him.

But he had tied my arms above my head, securing them to the wrought iron of my bed.

He had brought the silk ties himself—so considerate.

And then he had used another tie to cover my eyes, to lead me into this new trust exercise that I hadn't even known we'd be trying.

But he had been so gentle and sweet about it, yet so demanding.

And I had let him strip me bare, let him cover me with himself as he lapped and licked between my legs.

When he lifted his head, I heard him smack his lips together, and I smiled.

But then, he'd pierced me with two fingers, and I called out his name.

I called it out, but I couldn't hear it.

Had I screamed?

Or only moaned?

I couldn't see him, but I could feel him. His breath was on my neck, then my breasts, then between my legs as he lapped at me again, sucking and biting and playing with my clit. I came for him, and then he was inside me, one quick thrust that sent shockwaves of heat through my body. My nipples ached, more than they ever had before.

I wanted more, wanted him to fuck me hard into the bed until I screamed his name over and over again.

Tucker. Tucker. Tucker.

I opened my eyes, my hands between my legs, my panties long gone, my sheets a tangle on the edge of the bed. I froze.

"Dear God."

I slid my hand out from between my legs.

My clit was a hard nub, my lower lips swollen with need. But I refused to come right then.

I would not give myself an orgasm to a dream of Tucker Reinhard.

He was my brother's best friend. Yes, he had seen me virtually naked, and I had practically seen him naked. But I would not be having orgasmic dreams about him, thank you very much.

I found my panties tangled with my sheets and wiped my fingers, trying not to feel too embarrassed at how wet he'd gotten me just in my dreams.

It probably wasn't even Tucker.

He was simply the last guy I'd thought of before bed because I was thinking about dinner—not about having sex with him.

I was not going to have sex with Tucker. Ever.

Everything was fine. I wasn't losing my mind. And I did not want him.

It was only a weird dream. I was probably having sex with an Avenger or one of the Chrises while they were in my head.

I had a thing for Marvel, way more than DC. But then again, so did most of my friends. That was what happened when Marvel made the best movies.

And if I kept thinking about Marvel and Chris Evans versus Chris Hemsworth, I wouldn't actually stress the fuck out when it came to having a weird-ass dream about Tucker Reinhard.

Because I would not be having that dream again, thank you very much.

And I hadn't gotten myself off.

The fact that my nipples ached and my core kept pulsing as if I were right on the edge, seemed to mock me.

Of course, I was almost ready to come just at the thought of him.

Fuck that. It wasn't him. It was all a dream. All me. I had been the one having that dream, I did that.

Not Tucker. Oh, he might say he screwed with women, and he probably did with his dates, but none of them had stuck.

Maybe he was lousy in bed.

His lack of women had to be proof of him being totally lousy. Right?

I quickly jumped in the shower, turning the water to cold, and cursed his name as well as my own as I quickly washed my hair and body.

I washed between my legs and was quick about it. There would be no accidental clit touching.

There were rules about that.

At least, in my head.

I'd officially lost my mind. I wasn't sure if it had started before I professed my love to Tobey or after.

Who knew? I was over it all.

I hated the fact that Tobey had made me cry. That he had made me fall into myself and treated me like someone he didn't know.

I didn't know what would happen next with him, but what had happened to us already was a little concerning. While it was my fault in some ways, he had pushed me away, too. And I didn't know how we could come back from that. Or if we ever would.

I shrugged, trying to ignore the ache in my belly, and quickly pulled on my winter clothes, chilled even though I had the heat on blast.

But that's what happened when a cold snap hit Denver, and you were a landscape architect.

You had to double up on clothing and pray that things would work out well in the greenhouse.

Thankfully, I had a lot of paperwork to do today and a few meetings. Maybe if I were lucky, things would work out well, and I wouldn't have to be outside for too long. I loved the outdoors more than most anything in my life, but it was way too cold for that today.

There were reasons for the *colder than a witch's tit* saying, and I was grateful that I had worn two tanks under my Henley. Because, dear God. Apparently, it wasn't Tucker making my nipples hard, it was the breeze. See? I could laugh about it now. Not that I actually planned to tell him about that at all. I wasn't even sure I could face him with that kind of dream in my mind.

Silk scarves around my wrists? No, thank you. Claustrophobia much?

I grinned and shook my head, heading to work, trying to think about everything I had to do today.

Since it was the slow season, I was working alone most days, even though I had summer staff when needed. My brothers and Tobey helped out when they could. And that made me think of my former best friend again, and it hurt.

The fact that I had used the word *former* in my head?

Well, that was new.

I was so done worrying about my inept feelings. I wanted to focus on the good. My family was great, I had some amazing friends, and I'd had an incredible dream.

Okay, I was so not going to focus on that.

I went straight to work, finishing up two early meetings with people that I would eventually add as clients thanks to some wonderful referrals.

I couldn't wait for spring. That way, I could really get dirty and get things done. But the planning stages needed to be done, too, just like when it was hot as hell during the summer and things didn't want to grow because they were too shocked. I also had to deal with that.

By the time lunch rolled around, I was hungry and in desperate need of coffee.

I also had to get my things ready for a meeting with Erin and Zoey, since we were all working together on an upcoming wedding.

Erin was an amazing cake decorator, and Zoey was a florist.

I didn't always work with them when it came to weddings, but sometimes, we offered package deals because while Zoey worked with the flowers, outdoor weddings needed my special touch.

The fact that I could work with my two best friends made my job a little bit better.

And as if I had conjured them out of thin air, they walked in, both grinning from ear to ear.

"Hey there," I said, opening my arms as I gave them each a hug. I tried not to think about the last time I had seen them or what we had talked about: them setting me up on a date. It wasn't their fault that they wanted to help me get over Tobey. I wasn't sure if I could.

I hated that murky area between things that didn't make sense. But I was going to figure it all out.

I just had to remember to be happy.

"I thought I was meeting you guys at the coffee shop. Or was it at your cake shop?" I shook my head and looked down at my phone. "Okay, it was apparently at the bakery, and I was only thinking of coffee."

"Well, it seems we're all doing that because I really want a cup of coffee, too," Zoey said, looking around at the flowers I had put in the room.

Though they were my babies, she loved taking care of them, as well. Zoey was a fantastic florist who not only worked with cut flowers but also worked with potted plants.

She made sure that all plants lived their best lives or were showcased in the most amazing ways. Even if they had to be cut to do so.

I figured we were a match made in heaven.

"So, we came here to see if we could get you to come and get coffee rather than coming to my place," Erin said, looking down at her phone. "Devin says hi, by the way."

"Tell him hi," I said, looking at Zoey and rolling my eyes.

Zoey met my gaze, and we grinned, both of us shaking our heads.

The two lovebirds were a little ridiculous with each other, but if it put that look on Erin's face as well as a similar one on my brother's mug, I was happy.

Both of them deserved what they had, especially since my big brother had done so much for all of us without asking for anything for himself. And Erin had been through a really shitty marriage and a really crappy divorce. Finding a second chance with my brother meant everything in the world.

Now, if only we could get Zoey to be happy.

I was not going to include myself in that, thank you very much. Tried that, done that. I was done.

"So, you came here instead of texting me so we could get coffee?" I asked while pulling on my coat.

"You were on the way."

I nodded, smiling. "Are we taking two cars? Once we find parking and get out, it's going to be freezing as fuck."

"It's not that bad, and they actually have the heaters on along Main Street."

"Oh, that sounds amazing."

"How early did you get here if you didn't know they did that?" Zoey asked as we walked outside. I waved at one of my neighbors.

"Super early, apparently." I didn't add the bit about me waking up early because of my erotic dream. They really didn't need to know that.

"I've been craving coffee all day, and I only had a small cup for breakfast," I said, pushing thoughts of Tucker...and Tobey out of my mind.

"Good. Because I think I could probably drink an entire latte all by myself. I mean like the entire vat of it. Like every espresso bean in the place." I laughed at Zoey's words and made my way to my car, following them to our favorite café in Denver. It wasn't the closest place, but it was totally the best place.

We ordered our coffees, grinning at the woman with the cute blond bob behind the counter.

There was a tattoo shop next door, one that was owned by my sister-in-law's family. I'd always wanted to go in to get a tattoo. Maybe one day I would, but I was a little afraid.

I wasn't covered like Devin was, so maybe I should just get over my fears and get it done.

We took a corner seat and grinned at each other as we people-watched and talked about our upcoming business plans.

I loved this area. The fact that every type of person imaginable could walk in and get exactly what was perfect for them.

"I cannot wait to actually start working full-time on this wedding," Zoey said, taking out her tablet so we could look through her files. "You should really be a wedding planner in addition to being a florist," I said, looking at her notes.

"I love flowers too much for that. I love that idea, in that Nora Roberts' series, where all the women each had their own section of a whole wedding planning business. But I don't think that would work for us."

"You never know. We just need to meet someone who likes to organize everyone to insane degrees and then maybe find a photographer," Erin said.

"Tucker's good with a camera," I said, and then wanted to bite my tongue.

The girls met gazes, but I ignored it.

"And you know," I added, looking down at my phone so I wasn't actually looking at them, "Caleb is great at organizing everybody. Maybe he could be the wedding planner." I looked up as Erin laughed, and Zoey shrugged.

"What? It could happen."

"I really want to see your big brother talking about taffeta and lace."

I laughed at Zoey's words. "He'd be good at it."

"A former boilermaker who now works in construction? Sure, honey."

I shook my head at Zoey and took a sip of my coffee.

I looked over at Erin, who stiffened. I frowned.

"What is it?

"Shit," she whispered under her breath.

"Is it your ex?"

"No," Erin said, looking at Zoey. "But just know we didn't plan this. I'm sorry."

I frowned at both of them and then looked up as a very attractive blond man came walking up to us. He had tattoos down his forearms from what I could see peeking out of his Henley sleeves, and he was built like a quarterback. Broad shoulders, slender hips, and thick thighs.

He was sexy as hell and had a wicked grin.

But from the way Erin had whispered those words to me, I was a little afraid.

"Hey there. I was just thinking about you guys," the man said as he walked up to us.

"Jace. I didn't know you would be here," Erin said, and I could hear the honesty in her words, but I was still worried. I didn't know why, but if she seemed upset, I was afraid.

"I was over at Montgomery Ink getting my consult done. Walked over here for coffee, and saw you guys. Good to see you, too, Zoey." He turned to me and grinned. "And you must be Amelia." He smiled, and my stomach dropped.

Oh. So, he knew who I was. And from the way the girls kept looking at each other guiltily, I had a feeling I knew exactly what this was.

I wasn't going to get angry. My friends were just trying to be helpful, but I didn't want to be helped. All I wanted was to be okay and not pitied. I didn't want to be in a position where people tried to make me feel better. While it might make me a horrible person, I didn't want any of this. Why couldn't I be normal?

"Yes, I'm Amelia. I take it your name is Jace?"

"So, they've told you about me, too, have they?"

"No, can't say they have."

Why was this so awkward? Why did I hate it?

"Sorry, Jace," Erin said quickly, wringing her hands in front of her.

"We didn't actually mention to Amelia yet that we wanted to set her up on a blind date like this."

Like. *This*.

What the hell?

"Oh," Jace said quickly, his cheeks turning red.

"Sorry about that. They didn't actually say you would be here or anything. This is a total coincidence. But it's nice to meet you."

"It's nice to meet you, too. But I'm afraid they're mistaken."

I had no idea why the words were coming out of my mouth, but they seemed to be doing their own thing. "I'm already taken."

Zoey and Erin flipped their gazes to me, their eyes wide.

"Taken?" Zoey asked.

"By who?" Erin asked quickly.

Jace's brows rose, and he stuck his hands into his pockets. "Well, seems like I'm too late. Or not early enough, considering this wasn't supposed to actually be where I met you. Sorry for making things uncomfortable. I can head out."

Jace gestured over his shoulder, and I quickly slid out of the booth and shook my head. "You know what, I'm sorry. It's just been a weird couple of days. Or weeks. Anyway, it was so nice to meet you, Jace. But I am taken. He's a great guy. I like him."

Oh my God, why was I still talking? Why couldn't I shut up?

"Tucker's amazing," I continued, digging myself a deeper hole. "And it's all new, so my friends don't even know yet. But now they do. I hope you find someone great." I did not want to be pitied. They weren't pushing. They loved me. They didn't want me to be unhappy.

And I had been because of Tobey. They hadn't set this up.

And while this wasn't horrible, I hated this feeling. The oppressive weight that felt as if everything were pressing down on me, and even though they were trying to be kind, it was all too much.

So, I said Tucker's name. I shouldn't have. Why was his name the first one on my mind?

Why couldn't I have made up some random name?

Why did I have to create a fictional relationship with someone who was actually real?

There were places in hell for me. Dark ones.

And I deserved any punishment I got there.

"Well, it was nice to meet you. I hope we meet again though someday, just in case." He winked and then headed over to the door that connected the café to the tattoo shop. I turned to my friends, my eyes wide, "I need to go."

The girls opened their mouths, probably to ask questions, but I ignored them. I picked up my bag, turned on my heel, and ran.

Not because I didn't want to talk to them, though I really didn't. No, I took off because I had to head off Tucker before he heard.

Because, apparently, he was in a relationship with me. A new one, a secret one.

And he had no idea.

# Eight

*Tucker*

ONCE AGAIN, I GOT OUT OF THE SHOWER, exhausted. I'd worked the night shift, slept for a little bit of the morning, but then had to go back in for an emergency.

While I loved my job, I missed sleep at times.

When I got home, I'd wanted to go right back to sleep, but I knew I needed to stay up until at least eight since I had to work again today. I didn't usually work shifts like these, but I had been filling in for a friend who was getting married as well as having a baby, and that meant a little less sleep for me. As long as I did my best to regulate it a bit, I would be safe. And, honestly, that was really all that mattered.

I slid myself into my jeans, pulled a long sleeve t-shirt

over my head, and went into the kitchen to figure out what to eat.

The doorbell rang, and I frowned, wondering who it could be. Devin had said he had plans today with Erin, but I was pretty sure he was probably still working. He was still behind the desk following his accident, but he was doing better. It was strange to see him injured, the big man who never let anything knock him down. Except for a car. Apparently, a vehicle could take him out for a bit.

I opened the door, my eyes going wide.

"Hey. What are you doing here?" I asked Amelia, taking a step back. "Not that I'm not happy to see you, but I wasn't expecting you. Weren't you at work?"

"Yeah, well I had to take part of the day off. Long story. One that you're a part of."

My brows rose, but before I could ask anything about it, my phone buzzed from where it sat on the kitchen counter. "I need to look at that. Could be work."

"That's okay. Your work's important. I should go."

"You better not. You need to explain exactly why you're here because you're starting to freak me out. In a good way. You know I'm always here for you. I told you that. But you do need to explain. One sec." I picked up my phone and looked at the display, saw it was once again Melinda, and frowned. She had called before, but I hadn't called her back. Honestly, I'd forgotten, but I would do better this time. I'd call her back as soon as I could. But first, I had to figure out exactly why Amelia was here.

She was fidgeting, shifting her weight from side to side and biting her lip. Something was wrong. If it had anything to do with that fucker, Tobey, I was going to be pissed.

"I'd ask if you want a drink, but the last time I saw you do that, I had to hold your hair back as you threw up."

"I thought we weren't going to talk about that again." She pinched the bridge of her nose and started pacing in my foyer.

"Okay. How about some coffee?"

"I can't have coffee. I just had coffee. Coffee is the reason for all of this. I can probably never drink it again. Like I can never drink tequila again."

"Okay, hold up." I moved towards her, putting my hands on her shoulders to stop her.

She froze and looked up at me, her eyes wide. "I can't have coffee anymore."

"You said that already. And it's worrying." I put the back of my hand against her forehead, and she stuck her tongue out at me.

"I'm not sick. At least, I don't think so."

"Well, your face is warm, but mostly you look a bit frazzled."

"Just what everyone wants to hear. That they look frazzled."

"Frazzled isn't so bad. But you look like something's on

your mind. And between the pacing and the fact that you said you never want coffee again, I'm a little worried about you."

"You should be worried. I think I messed things up."

My brows rose again, and then I gently nudged her towards my couch.

She took a seat before standing up again, pacing around a bit, then sitting right back down.

I figured she'd probably do this for a bit because whenever Amelia was nervous or needed to formulate her thoughts, she paced.

I had forgotten that for a moment, but now it all came back to me. I'd known Amelia for years. Things were a little different now, but they weren't *too* different. I needed to remind myself of that every once in a while.

I took a seat in the corner of my sectional and sat back, watching her move.

She was really beautiful, even when she was tugging at her hair, causing it to fall out of its braid and tumble over her shoulders.

Her face was a little red from the outdoors, and probably from her nerves regarding whatever else was going through her mind.

She was in her work clothes, so that meant jeans and a long-sleeved t-shirt, but the outfit worked for her. She pulled off dresses and other outfits fine, too—something I'd told myself I wasn't going to think about.

Because that would be wrong. So wrong.

"I have a proposition for you," she blurted out, and I froze, looking up at her.

I swallowed hard, trying not to think about what she could mean. Because she couldn't possibly mean any of the things that were going through my mind right now. Mostly because my thoughts had nothing to do with clothes, and everything to do with her being on her knees. Or me being on mine. Or either of us doing things to the other that would probably be illegal in some states.

Okay, enough of that.

"A proposition."

"Yeah. That's not a great word. I have an offer. No, that's not a great word either. An idea. Yes, an idea. And I need your help."

Intrigue piqued, I leaned forward, my forearms on my knees. "Okay, an offer. An idea. You need my help. Well, I said I would be here for anything you need. But if you're going to start with the word *proposition*, I'm going to need some details."

"I need you to be my beard."

I blinked, tilting my head to look at her. "I have a beard. A small one, but I don't shave every day. Though I don't actually know what you mean by that. Do you need me to grow a beard? I can do that, but I don't like it to get too shaggy."

She threw her hands up and growled.

Why was that so sexy?

"No, I need you to be *my* beard."

"You're growing a beard?"

"Oh my God. I need you to be my fake boyfriend. Like a beard?"

I shook my head, wondering why that made no sense. Because, what the fuck?

"Excuse me?"

"Hear me out."

"Oh, I'm going to. And then we're going to sit down, and I'm going to force some coffee on you. Because this must be one of the side effects of you not having coffee."

"I've had coffee today. And that's my problem."

"Well, maybe we'll give you some fucking decaf. A fake boyfriend? And isn't the term *beard* like the exact opposite of what you're doing? And antiquated?"

"Maybe. But we're making it ours. And people totally use it."

"Not in common conversation. Hence why I had no idea what you actually meant. Are you insane? Devin is my best friend."

"Yes. And that's a problem."

"My best fucking friend."

And, yeah, I had come really hard thinking about her, but I wasn't going to say that. In fact, it never needed to be said. We would never mention that to Devin. Ever. Because I liked my nuts exactly where they were.

"Okay, I didn't really think it out. You were just the first person I thought of." A lovely blush spread over her cheeks, and I had to wonder exactly why I was the first person to come to mind and not Tobey.

I did not want to preen at that. I would not preen at that.

What the fuck was wrong with me?

"Okay, I need you to explain exactly what happened. Use small words and go slowly. Short sentences. Why the fuck do you need a fake relationship? Is it because of Tobey? Because you don't need to prove anything to that fuckhead or anyone else."

"Stop calling him names."

"He made you cry. I can call him whatever the fuck I want." I hadn't meant to put that much vehemence in my tone, but her eyes widened, and her mouth parted.

"Sorry. He made you cry. And I'm not okay with that. I don't like how he treated you, and I don't like the way you keep beating yourself up over it. You're allowed to have feelings. You're allowed to love somebody." Not that I thought it was actually love, but I was in no way qualified to go into someone's feelings. For all I knew, Amelia really loved the asshole.

"Tucker."

"Don't *Tucker* me. I don't like the way he treated you. So, he's always going to be an asshole in my eyes. You do not need to bring up a fake relationship and pretend that you're happy or doing better than he is or whatever you're trying to do here. You simply need to be yourself, and that will prove that. He'll see what he's missing. Because he knows he's missing a damn fine thing with you. And not just being your friend. You know that. Everybody should know that."

I hadn't meant to say all that. And from the look in her eyes, she hadn't expected me to say it either.

Well, good. It seemed I was crossing all the lines. Might as well be her fake boyfriend, too, right?

No. Because if I did that, my cock would want to do the thinking. And that was not something I could allow. Ever.

"It's not about Tobey. Well, it is, but it's not *for* Tobey. Let me explain."

"You better, or I really am going to give you that fucking coffee."

She laughed and shook her head. She put her hands on her head, then moved them over her face and screamed into them.

"Feel better?"

"A little."

"Good. Because if you don't mind, I might do the same in a little bit if you don't explain."

She grinned, and it went to her eyes this time. Look at that. Progress. I only had to act like a complete fool to make her happier. That was good to know. I liked happy Carrs. They were my family. Amelia was practically my sister.

And I really needed to remember that.

"Okay. This is what happened. Everybody has been so accommodating. Not you. Well, you've been accommodating, too, and you've been sweet. But you've also been fun. A little more in your face than usual with me, but you've always been a great guy. And you're treating me like normal. Like a friend."

"Of course, I am. That's what I said I was going to do."

She didn't need to know about my dreams. Didn't need to know that I'd jacked off thinking about her. Because that was horrible. And I wasn't going to do it again.

I hadn't done it again.

I would not do it again later, either, damn it.

"Well, not everyone's the same. Oh, they try to be. But I see the pity. They want to help and make me feel better. Well, my brothers are a little different. The three of them just want to growl and beat the shit out of Tobey."

"And I'm okay with that."

"Tucker."

"What? I'm only being honest here."

"Anyway," she said, clearly exasperated with me. Good, because I was feeling pretty much the same. "It's Erin and Zoey."

"What did they do?" I asked, a little worried.

"They're amazing. I love them. And they just want me to be happy, but I think they got it in their heads that I would be happiest if I got over Tobey."

My brows rose straight to my hairline. "And?"

"And they talked about me to some guy named Jace."

"Jace, wait. I know that name." I frowned, trying to think back. "Tall guy, wide shoulders, blond hair, and tattoos?"

"You know him?"

"Yeah, he's a firefighter. Great guy." And I kind of hated him a little. Why did I hate him?

"Well, that's good. Anyway, I don't know how it happened, but the girls were talking to him and mentioned me and said they wanted to set us up on a blind date."

Now I wanted to rip Jace's head from his body.

That was a strange reaction. I didn't do serious relationships. I didn't do relationships at all. That meant that whatever the fuck was going on with me right then had nothing to do with Amelia. I was clearly losing my damn mind.

"So, you don't want to go on a date with him?" I asked, cautious.

"No. I don't know. I just want some time. And I know it's stupid. I should've simply said that I wasn't ready to date. They would've understood. But I didn't. Instead, I said I was dating someone." And then it clicked.

"You said you were dating me." I looked down at my phone, a little afraid that Devin hadn't called me. Maybe he was already on his way with a hatchet.

That's what happened in movies, right? Hell, maybe I should change my address.

"Everything's going to be fine. But I need you to

pretend for a little bit. We'll make sure everyone knows it's casual. I need to figure out what I want, and I can't do that if everybody's worrying about me."

"Amelia."

"Please. I'm tired of the pity. You don't pity me."

"Because you don't need it. You need to kick his ass."

"Thanks for that. But, seriously. Go out with me."

"Amelia."

"I'm not saying sex."

I paused. Grinning. I couldn't help it. "No sex?" I purred.

"Tucker."

"I'm just saying. Sex could help." I was not thinking about having sex with her. Totally not thinking about it. Yes, I was thinking about it. Horrible.

"Okay, Tucker. I really need your help. I'm tired. I want to feel normal again."

I ran my hands through my hair and then screamed into them as she had earlier. She let out a forced laugh, and then I stood up and paced like she had before.

"If I do this, and that's a big fucking *if*, that means you have to let me hold your hand. You have to let me be near you. You're going to make me act like something we're not in front of my best friends. You're basically forcing me to lie to him. My best fucking friend and the rest of the family I chose for myself. And I don't know what to do about that. Because you want a fake relationship? How far does that go?

Are we only dating in front of them? Will we go on dates where people actually see us? Or post on social media? What does all of this mean?"

"I don't know. I don't know anything. I just said it, and now I have to deal with it. I'll tell them I lied."

I was making a stupid choice. This was such a stupid decision. But I hated seeing her like this.

If it helped her, I'd be fine. Devin would understand—at least he would later. We would explain everything to him once she'd had some time. He would get it. He had to.

"I should pick someone else."

I leveled my gaze on her and growled, "No. It will be me."

Fuck, what was wrong with me?

"Because I don't want anyone else taking advantage of you," I added. See, that was fine.

"Okay. We can do this. For a little bit. Until I feel normal. And then we'll explain to everyone what happened. They won't be angry. They can't be. I don't want them to be mad at you."

"I'll do this," I said again, "but I want something in return."

"What?" she asked, clearly leery.

"I don't know yet."

"Well, that sounds dangerous."

I looked at her then, knowing we were probably making a horrible mistake. But if she needed this, I'd figure out a way to make it work. Her brothers would understand eventually. They would realize that their little sister needed some space, and if I had to be the person to help her with that, then I would be.

I just hoped that nobody got hurt in the fallout.

"Amelia, baby, all of this is dangerous."

Though I had a feeling she wasn't the one in the line of fire this time.

# NINE

*Amelia*

"WHAT WAS I THINKING?"

Oh. That's right. I hadn't been thinking. I'd been overwhelmed and did some stupid shit. That's what happened when you didn't think things through. Instead of acting like a rational adult, someone who made reasonable decisions, I had thrown out a fake relationship that would probably fuck everything up.

*Great going, Amelia. You're totally winning at life.*

"I can do this. It's not going to be a big deal. It's only a little date. Not even a real one."

Why was I even talking to myself in the mirror?

Oh, yeah, because Tucker would be here any minute to pick me up for our fake date. One that wouldn't even be a real date because we'd be with my family.

Because, of course, I, Amelia Carr, had to have my first fake date with my fake boyfriend at a family barbecue. All because I needed to show him around and act like everything was fine, and everything was cool, and nothing is going to go crazy.

That was so not right.

I was clearly losing my mind, especially if I kept talking to myself. Someone was probably going to show up and take me away.

Then there would be nothing left. Only an empty shell of the person that once was. A life full of meaningless choices and horrible mistakes.

Great, now I just needed to wax poetic and call it a day.

I was pretty sure that Devin had orchestrated this whole family barbecue thing as a way to figure out exactly what was going on with Tucker and me, but I wasn't sure.

The fact that he hadn't even asked me about it since Erin and Zoey found out, worried me. What would happen to Tucker once the two of them were alone?

And what would happen to us if he found out the truth?

Because they needed to know the truth. I didn't know if I could tell them tonight, though. I hated lying to them. But I also didn't want to feel like the defunct baby sister who kept making mistakes, over and over again. I just wanted a little time where I could feel like I was doing something right.

But I was happy, and I was getting over Tobey, and everything was fine. The fact that I didn't think about Tobey every five minutes anymore or even as my best friend meant something. Maybe I was getting better. Perhaps I was healing. But I needed more time without those pitying looks.

And if Tucker could help me, then I would deal with the consequences. And I would do everything in my power to make sure *he* didn't have to deal with them.

The doorbell rang, and I quickly looked myself over in the mirror one more time, making sure that my boots were zipped up to my knees, and my boobs weren't too far out of my shirt. I didn't need to actually show the goods on this date because...number one, it wasn't a date. And number two, it was Tucker. Plus, going to a family event looking like a hooker probably wasn't the best idea.

Not that I ever looked like a hooker, but...

I ran towards the door and opened it, letting out a relieved breath that Tucker was actually here. I'd been a little worried that he would say no at the last minute and cancel. I honestly wouldn't have blamed him.

"You made it."

Tucker stuck his hands into his jeans' pockets and shrugged, looking far hotter than he should. I couldn't help but notice the way his thighs filled out his jeans, or how his leather jacket hugged his broad shoulders. I really needed to stop looking at him like that. It wasn't good for me, wasn't good for either of us. And the back and forth in my mind was going to give me a complex. I already had enough of those.

"I said I'd be here. So, here I am. Are you sure you want to do this?"

"I don't know. I think I have to."

"You don't have to do anything you don't want to do. Seriously. You want to hang out here and ignore everything? We can totally do that."

"No, I can't. I love my family. And they love me."

"Then why do I need to be your beard, Amelia?"

"Now you're using the word."

He stepped into the house even though I hadn't actually invited him in. That's what happened when I was a little off. I became rude.

"I don't know. I don't want them to worry about me. Can I just have a minute where I don't have to keep being that sister?"

"They don't think of you like that. They love you."

"You say that, and yet they were the ones always worried that I was making a mistake by not being with Tobey. Or by being with him. And then look what happened."

"But that's not your fault."

"We can agree to disagree that it was sort of my fault."

He sighed. "I'm here for you. I said I would be. Just make sure you put ice on my bruises once your brother kicks my ass."

"He's not going to hurt you," I said quickly, wincing. "Though he might. He's strong. I really should have used someone else."

Tucker narrowed his eyes. "No. You shouldn't have. Because someone else would have taken advantage. And I won't do that. I'm just going to make sure that everyone knows you're fine and that we're keeping this casual. And that I am in no way going to hurt their precious baby sister."

For some reason, that sent warm flutters down into my stomach, but I quickly brushed them away. I put on my leather jacket and pulled my purse over my shoulder. "I really wish they would stop calling me their precious baby sister. I'm not precious."

Tucker reached out and slid a piece of hair behind my shoulder, the wisp of it delicate on my skin. He was so gentle with me. As if I were indeed precious. "Baby, you are. At least, to them."

I looked at his eyes, swallowing hard. Damn it. He was really good at that smooth-talking thing. No wonder all the women fell for him. Wasn't going to be me, though. No, thank you.

"Okay. Let's just get this over with," I said quickly, pushing past him to the door.

"Not so fast," he said, putting his hand on the door to block me.

"What? Did I forget something?"

"Yeah. Like how we're dating. The story. How many lies I'm supposed to tell my best friend. Because I really shouldn't be lying to him at all, you know."

I heard the guilt in his voice, and I knew he was doing this for me. Only I didn't know why. And that worried me. But then I remembered the looks on everyone's faces. The pity. And it was just a little lie. Maybe if we went on enough fake dates, it would even become real. At least in terms of the technicalities. Because there would be no feelings involved. We were already casual. A little more wouldn't be that far off the mark.

"I don't know. Maybe keep it as real as possible?"

"So...say I saw your boobs after you threw up and couldn't keep my hands off you?"

Yes, completely deadpan.

I put my hands on my face and screamed into them. "Oh my God. We're never telling that story."

"Mmm, I might. Maybe not to your brothers because they may actually kill me, but to someone." He grinned as I lowered my hands and punched him in the stomach.

Sadly, I only hurt my hand, he was that solid. I shook it off. "How many days do you work out? It's ridiculous. Don't you have a full-time job?"

"I do. One that I put in far too many hours for." He

rubbed his stomach and then smiled. I hated that smile. Actually, maybe I kind of liked it. "I'm just blessed with good genes, though I do work out a lot. But, okay. We'll go with part of the truth. I can do that. You had a bad day, got drunk, I took care of you, and things progressed slowly from there. So we're casual. Friends who hang out."

"That's fine. And that's really almost totally the truth. We are friends."

"Even though you said you were dating me."

"Well, yes. But that's only a little addition. It's not too crazy. Right?"

"Sure, hon. Whatever you say."

"Why are you doing this?"

He looked into my eyes, and I didn't know what he saw there. I couldn't read him, but I'd never been able to read Tucker. He was always the nice guy, the one that could make anyone smile, the one who would always be there for you. But I didn't know much more about him. I only knew facts. I didn't know *him*. So, I didn't know why he was doing this. But I honestly didn't know why I was doing this either.

"Let's just make sure they know I'm okay, and then we can end it slowly. No hard feelings. No one needs to beat you up because it's just casual, and we'll make sure that they know we've never had sex."

He snorted, shaking his head. "Yeah, your brothers

CARRIE ANN RYAN

know how I am with women. They're probably going to guess that we've slept together."

"Okay, we'll make sure they know. I'll tell them."

"So you're going to tell your brothers that we've never had sex. They're not going to believe you."

"They'll know. As will the others. They'll know that we've never had sex."

"But, like you said, I did see your boobs."

"Oh, shut up. We're not talking about that."

"And you saw me in a towel. And that's practically naked."

I pushed those thoughts out of my mind. I would not be thinking about that ever again. Except for in my dreams. No, not even there. God, I had to stop thinking about that. And everything else that came to mind when I thought of Tucker. What was wrong with me?

"Okay. Enough of that. They'll know, everyone will know. We're only casual. And that's totally not a lie. Because it's what we are. We've eaten together. We're going to family events together. It's practically the truth."

"Okay. I'll make sure that nobody gives you pitying looks. And ensure they think you can make your own choices without making mistakes. Because I know you're worried about that. And when the time comes, we'll say you ended it, and that it was completely casual, and I never touched you. How's that?"

"Sounds like a plan. The perfect plan, right?" I knew my

voice was a little high when I asked that last part because it was totally not the right thing to say. But I was already going down this wrong-decision path, I might as well keep going. After all, I had shown my boobs to Tobey, and then to Tucker. Might as well keep piling my bad decisions on top of one another.

"You're going to be okay," he said, slowly running his fingers down my cheek. I froze, and he just clucked his tongue.

"Okay, you have to stop doing that."

"Stop doing what?" I asked, my voice oddly breathy. That wasn't good.

"Don't flinch or freeze when I touch you. They're going to know everything's a lie, and then they're going to wonder why you're lying."

"Well, how much touching are you going to do in front of my family?" I asked quickly.

"Not that much. But I might want to hold your hand." He lifted his hand from my cheek, ran it down my arm, and then slid his fingers through mine.

I swallowed hard, but then laughed when he grinned at me, giving my hand a squeeze.

"See? You're doing fine. You're getting used to my touch."

"Not too used to it. Remember, we're not doing the whole sleeping with each other thing."

"Oh, I know. Don't worry."

He gave my hand one more squeeze, leaned down, and kissed me on the tip of the nose. Then he led the way out of my house.

I had no idea how I had put myself in such a situation, I only knew that if it had to be with anyone, I was glad that it was Tucker. I trusted him. I just hoped he wouldn't get hurt because of my choices.

By the time we got to the house, we were the last people there. I'd kind of wanted to slide in without anybody noticing, but it wasn't like we were a huge group. Dimitri and Thea weren't able to make it because they had a Montgomery family dinner, so that meant it would only be the three Carrs plus Erin and now Tucker. Zoey was coming as well since everybody had wanted it to be even, but I wasn't going to touch that idea with a ten-foot pole. Plus, Zoey was a friend, so it wasn't really *even*. In terms of couples anyway.

"Okay. We can do this. It's not going to be too hard. We can totally do this."

"Are you talking to me or yourself?" Tucker asked as I opened the door without knocking. He wasn't holding my hand but was standing near me. As soon as we walked in, everyone was suddenly there. Caleb and Zoey were glaring at one another in the middle of some conversation, but they turned to look as we walked in. Erin and Devin were whispering in the other corner, nearly kissing, but they paused to look over at us, too.

Oh, good. This wasn't awkward at all.

"You're here. Good. Want to come into the kitchen for a minute?" Devin asked, throwing his thumb over his shoulder. "Got a question for you, Tucker."

"Yep, we're here. And we brought potato salad."

I held up the dish I had grabbed on the way out and tried to smile.

"I made it myself. I promise it isn't store-bought this time."

"I told you that you didn't need to bring anything," Erin said.

She grinned but took the dish from me. "I mean, I already made everything for the sides. Especially since it's winter and we're not actually going to barbecue."

"I will have you know that I can go out there shirtless in jeans right now, woman." Devin slapped her on the ass, and she glared over her shoulder at him. I rolled my eyes, laughing.

And then Tucker stepped all the way into the house, right up to my side. And the room got quiet again. Good. This wasn't going to be awkward at all. Why was I doing this again? Oh, yeah, I didn't actually have a good reason.

"I'm just going to get this out of the way. You hurt her, I'll kick your ass. I don't know what's going on here, but I promised her I would stop getting in the way of her dates a long time ago. That's why I never filleted Tobey like I wanted to."

"Devin," I growled.

"What? Dimitri's not here. Therefore, I am the eldest, and therefore, I can do this."

"I'm here, too," Caleb growled, taking a sip of his beer. "And I really want to see what happens. This is going to be fun, isn't it?" He gave me a weird look that I couldn't really decipher, and I winced.

"Let's just forget it. We're here to eat and have fun. Tucker's been to tons of these things. Nothing's different."

"Sure. Whatever you say." Devin stormed off, and I had no idea if he was angry at me, Tucker, or someone else.

"I'm going to go follow him," Tucker said quickly.

"You don't have to," I whispered.

"Yeah, I do. You can come with if you want, Caleb."

"I think I will," Caleb said, tipping his beer in Zoey's direction. She flipped him off. Well, tonight was going to be interesting.

"So, how did that go?" Erin asked, wincing.

"About as bad as it could."

"No, it could have been worse," Zoey said. "Tobey could have shown up." She smiled as she said it, and I knew she was trying to make things a bit more normal, and I was grateful for it.

Because Tobey had been a big part of all of our lives, and he wasn't here now. I didn't know what that meant. But Tucker *was* here. And I was fine. Everything would be fine.

Dinner actually went reasonably well, everybody pretty much ignoring the massive elephant in the room. Whether the elephant was Tucker and me, or Tobey and me, I didn't know. Maybe it was a herd of elephants, all quietly stampeding around.

By the time we finished dinner and everybody was cleaning up, I found myself alone at the sink with Caleb. "I know you're lying, baby girl. But I get it. Just don't get hurt. And don't hurt him."

My eyes widened, and I looked over at him.

"What are you talking about?" I asked, my pulse racing.

"I've always been able to tell when you're lying. Mostly to get out of little things when we were younger. Devin and Dimitri weren't as good as that. But I was more of a hell-raiser than you were. So, I understand. I figure you need some time where nobody's making you feel bad about Tobey, and that's okay. Don't fuck each other over when you're trying to figure out what you want, though. All right?"

I nodded, swallowing hard as I kept my eyes on my dishes. I didn't want to hurt Tucker. He was so strong and good at hiding things that sometimes I forgot that he'd been hurt as a kid. I should end this now. Only I didn't know how.

I shouldn't have opened my mouth at all with the girls and Jace. I should have told everyone that I was fine. But I had tried that before, and it hadn't worked.

"I'll be okay," I whispered.

"Good."

Caleb didn't say anything else, just helped me dry things until we were done, then I walked back out to the living room. That was where I heard Devin and Tucker talking.

"You hurt my sister, I'll kill you."

Tucker nodded before I got a chance to say anything. "Got it. I'm not risking you guys. I'm not risking my family because of this. Okay?"

Jesus Christ, I was a horrible person. We were his family. He had no one else, and I was using him.

I needed to stop this. I needed to be honest and break it off because I refused to hurt him. I should be the one hurting, not him. But then he met my gaze and gave me a slight shake of his head, and I didn't say anything.

He was *so* good.

And I was a horrible person.

We said our goodbyes, and I was quiet in the car on the way home, not sure what to say. By the time we reached my house, I could barely swallow, though I tried to be okay. But I really wasn't.

Tucker walked me to the door and then walked me all the way inside as I tried to sort through my thoughts and feelings.

"Okay, that wasn't so bad."

I blinked at him. "It sucked."

"Maybe." I shrugged and looked off into the distance as I tried to calm my heart.

"I know my payment," he said softly.

Payment? "What?"

"My payment. For this. For all of this. I know what it should be."

"Okay. Do you want money or something? You make more than I do. But I can get you money."

He smiled. "I don't want money. Every date? Every lie we tell? I get to kiss you."

I froze, my throat going dry.

"What?" I asked, but then I couldn't think at all. Because Tucker lowered his head, and his lips were on mine.

# TEN

*Tucker*

No, I shouldn't be doing this.

Yes, it was a mistake.

But, damn it.

I wasn't going to stop.

I couldn't.

Amelia's mouth under mine was even better than in my dreams and fantasies.

And I'd had a whole fucking lot of them when it came to this mouth.

I wasn't going to say this was the best feeling, the best kiss I'd ever had. Because while part of me, a deeply hidden part that would never be looked upon again, might think that, there was no way I could let myself actually believe that in truth.

Because if I did, then this kiss would be something more than it should be.

This was only a deal.

Just a payment.

Nothing more.

But it sure as hell wasn't anything less.

I had my hands on either side of her face, tilting her head back ever so slightly so I could deepen the kiss. She tasted of coffee and sweetness and a temptation that I damn sure should ignore.

Only I couldn't.

And I had a feeling that could and would be my downfall.

I pulled away, knowing I should have done it sooner.

"What...what was that?" she asked, her voice breathy.

I didn't know.

"My payment."

She looked at me, her brows furrowed. "You kissed me. Why did you kiss me? That wasn't part of the deal."

I lowered my head to her face and took a step back. Then I stuffed my hands into my pockets and rocked back on my heels. "No, it wasn't. But I figure we should try."

"This can't change anything, Tucker."

It didn't hurt to hear her say that. Because I didn't want

it to change anything either. But I had to kiss her. It might have been wrong for both of us, but I had to do it.

"Of course, it won't change anything. That's fine with me." That wasn't a lie.

"So, you're telling me you're going to kiss me every time, but we have to pretend we're dating for my family?" she asked, sounding a little incredulous.

"Maybe." She looked at me, and I sighed. "Amelia, it doesn't have to mean anything. We're friends."

"Friends who kiss."

"And are fake-dating. I'm your beard, remember?"

"I can't tell if you're joking or not."

"A little. But not really. I wanted to kiss you. I can't help that. And I figured...why not?"

"Because I'm still not over Tobey."

I didn't know why that hurt so much. It shouldn't. But I'd just have to get over it. Because it wasn't like I wanted Amelia in that way. Sure, I wanted to kiss her. But I couldn't let it become anything else. It wasn't smart for either of us.

"So, you're going to kiss me whenever we go on a fake date?" she repeated.

"Yeah. Unless you really don't want that. If that's true, I'll never do it again. I'll never force you into anything, Amelia. I hope you know that."

She looked at me for so long, I had a feeling it was Amelia who didn't want to hide or apologize. But then she spoke.

"Okay. I can do that." She blushed so prettily that I wanted to reach out and touch her cheek, but I knew that would be a bad decision for both of us. Instead, I leaned in and kissed the tip of her nose like I always did and smiled. "Until our next fake date."

"Or until we see each other as friends. Because that's not going to change, right, Tucker?"

I looked into her eyes and tried to figure out what she was thinking. The fact that I didn't know what *I* was thinking probably didn't help matters. "Yeah. Always." And then I walked out and hoped like hell I hadn't made another mistake.

The next morning, I woke up hard again, but I didn't get myself off. Doing so would likely make me think of Amelia, and I didn't want to cross that line again.

I couldn't be that big of an asshole. At least not again.

I showered quickly and got ready for work, then frowned when the doorbell rang.

I wasn't expecting any deliveries. But for all I knew, I had gotten drunk and Primed again.

I opened the door and cursed.

Of course, the Carr brothers were here.

All three of them. Dimitri, Devin, and Caleb.

"Hey, mind if we come in?" Devin asked, pushing his way in.

Caleb just gave me a smirk, and Dimitri flashed me an apologetic smile.

Well, at least this was going to be an interesting way to start the day.

"So, I figure you need to talk?" I asked, trying to sound casual. I closed the door behind them, keeping the heat in, and turned to face them.

"Yeah. We'd better talk." Caleb folded his arms over his chest as Dimitri leaned against the wall, and Devin started to pace.

"What the fuck is going on, man?" Devin asked, glaring as he continued pacing.

"Just what we told you. We're friends." I couldn't lie. Not totally. I wasn't that good at it. I had been better when I was younger, but that had been for survival. But lying to Devin? I really wasn't good at it. And I shouldn't be.

"Okay, then. You're dating."

"More like seeing each other while still friends."

Devin shook his head and came straight at me. I stiffened but didn't move my hands up. If Devin needed to hit me, I probably deserved it. After all, in his mind, I was defiling his baby sister. I deserved whatever I got.

"I couldn't get involved in her and Tobey's relationship. I promised her that I would never do anything like that. But she's my baby sister, and you're my fucking best friend. So, I'm already in the middle of it."

Shame crawled through me, and then I remembered that kiss, and the fact that I'd already had dreams about her.

The idea that it wasn't as much of a lie as it should be rankled, but it made it easier for me to face him.

Maybe that's why I'd kissed Amelia the night before. Because I needed it to be true. Perhaps not only for me, but for the friendship that'd meant the world to me my entire life.

"I'm not going to hurt her."

"You know, I really want to believe that," Devin said. "But I don't know what to believe anymore. I didn't even know you and she saw each other that way."

I ignored the pain that comment caused. "I'm not going to hurt her," I repeated. "We're only friends."

"Friends that seem to be a bit more," Dimitri said, shaking his head. "Not that I was actually there. It's just what I heard."

"We're friends, dating casually. She needs to be okay and have some fun while she's getting over Tobey. And I'm that guy, remember? The one you can have fun with."

Why did that statement sound so weird?

Caleb shook his head, and I had to wonder what the other man was thinking. Caleb usually saw too much, but I didn't know what he saw now.

"I'm not going to hurt her," I whispered. It had to be true. Because we were friends. Friends who might want each other sexually, that much was evident, but we weren't going to let it be anything more.

After all, she was still in love with Tobey.

And I couldn't love anyone.

She needed me to stand in the way of her family and everyone else so she could have a moment to just be. To think. And I could be that guy for her. I didn't think I could be anything else.

"You don't hurt women," Devin said, his shoulders lowering a fraction. "I know you. You go through them, but not the way everyone thinks. You're a good man. But you fucking hurt my sister, I'll kick your ass. Because I couldn't do that for Tobey, but I can for you."

I shook my head. "Thanks." I laughed as I said it, and Caleb rolled his eyes. Dimitri winced.

"Don't thank me. Just take care of her. Because even though I keep saying 'don't hurt her' and all that shit, I don't want her to hurt you either. You deserve good things, Tucker. And my sister's the best. So, I hope it really fucking works out."

I stood there shocked as Devin reached out, squeezed my shoulder, and then nodded at his brothers. The three of them walked out of the house, leaving me standing there alone, and now probably late to work.

What the fuck just happened? Was that a blessing?

Because it sure as hell sounded like a blessing. But that couldn't be right. Because I was not right for Amelia. And this was a fake relationship. I was her beard, for God's sake. We couldn't be anything more to each other. That was how it had to be.

That's what I needed it to be.

I shook my head and then made my way back to my bedroom so I could get the rest of my things and try to make it to work on time.

I had a long day ahead of me, and I needed to keep my mind on my patients, my files, and not on Amelia. But it was really hard when it came to her.

Everything seemed to be these days.

I worked a ten-hour shift, my eyes crossing by the end of it, but it was good work. I hadn't been able to think about anyone but the people in front of me, and what they needed. There had been some bad cases, things that I needed to wash off and try to forget for a moment. Because while I could be in the moment with my patients and think about things clinically, I couldn't take it home with me.

That might make me a bad person, but the things that I saw? No, I couldn't bring it home every day and still be okay. The people that were sick had to bring it home, and I would always think of them, but I couldn't be that person. I couldn't be the person who lived it day in and day out in so many ways where I could still be human in the end. Because while at work, those people and their problems layered upon one another, and it ended up drowning me in everything all at once.

It was the way I dealt with things. It might not be the healthiest, but I knew I wasn't alone in doing it.

Having things in little boxes in my mind helped me figure out how to make it through each day.

It helped me think about what I needed to be me.

I had to stop by the grocery store on my way home since I was completely out of vegetables, and I didn't really want to live on burgers and fries—even though that sounded really fucking good.

Thankfully, I didn't get hit on in the produce aisle as I had been prone to over the past few weeks. Maybe they saw that there was an *off-limits* sign on me now.

I frowned, pausing as I picked up some broccoli. Off-limits? Since when was I off-limits?

But maybe I was. I couldn't be with anyone else if I were even in a somewhat realistic relationship with Amelia. That wasn't fair to her, and it would probably get my ass kicked by her brothers immediately. So I wasn't going to look at anyone else. I wouldn't even bother going on a date. Because I was protecting Amelia.

And myself.

It had nothing to do with any feelings.

Not at all.

I got to my car and put my groceries in, and then froze as I noticed the man two cars down.

Huh. I knew that guy. I knew him really fucking well. Or I thought I had.

"Tobey," I growled out, hitting the button on my trunk so the door would close as I walked over to him.

Tobey's eyes widened, and my fists clenched at my sides. Oh, I was going to jail tonight. I was going to punch his lights out. Though he didn't deserve that. Oh, I might want to kick his ass, but I wouldn't. I didn't think with my fists, even though I really wanted to at the moment.

"Hey, Tucker. What's up?" Tobey spoke quickly, closing his trunk before he stuffed his hands into his pockets.

That definitely wasn't the best stance if you thought you were going to be on the receiving end of a punch.

But Tobey probably didn't think he did anything wrong. After all, it wasn't like he and Amelia had ever dated. Contrary to what everybody who saw them thought.

But it really wasn't about the dating. It was about the friendship thing. They had been best fucking friends. And he'd screwed her over.

The fact that I felt like I was doing something similar to Devin probably didn't help my attitude.

"What the fuck is wrong with you?" I growled out, anger pouring through my veins.

"What do you mean?"

"How the hell could you do that to Amelia?" I really shouldn't be doing this. This was none of my business. But, technically, I was lying to my best friends and in a fake relationship with Amelia because of this asshole. So, maybe I should let my rage out on him.

After all, it was either that or yell at myself. And I'd already done enough of that.

"I didn't do anything to Amelia. She's the one who did something to me."

Oh, he was really lucky we were in public, or I would have kicked his ass. Because while Tobey was broad and had some muscle, I was a better fighter. Tobey didn't have grit. I might smile more, but I could definitely kick this mother-fucker's ass.

And every time I looked at that little wimpy smile on his face, it made me want to hit him more.

Over and over.

Fucking asshole.

"Excuse me?"

"She's the one who went and reacted like that. I'm sorry she thought the wrong thing. That she thought she loved me, or that I could love her. It's not the case. She just had to be her normal self. Overdramatic."

What the fuck? Wasn't this guy supposed to be her best friend? Who the hell talked like that about someone they loved? Even if it wasn't romantic love, there had to be some-thing about this guy that made her love him. But all I could see was nothing. I saw a useless sack of a man who didn't deserve anything that Amelia felt. Not that I could actually tell Amelia that. Because she wouldn't believe me. Because love was blind.

And I wanted nothing to do with that.

"What the fuck is wrong with you?" I whispered, shaking my head.

"There's nothing wrong with me. I'm sorry she thought the wrong thing. And once Beth is okay with what happened, I'll be back. You know she was my friend. And I hated hurting her. But things are weird now. And I don't want to damage things with Beth."

"You led Amelia on. She loved you. You had to know that. Hell, even I saw it."

"Sure, but I didn't really think anything of it. You know? I figured it was just one of those puppy-love things because I was the only guy who was ever around. Well, other than you. But you don't really count."

I was not going to hit this man. I was not going to hit this man.

I had to keep repeating that. Because I needed my hands for work. And going to jail and needing Devin to bail me out probably wouldn't help matters. Oh, he would gleefully do it, especially if I kicked Tobey's ass. But still, not a good thing.

And Tobey was the kind of guy who'd probably press charges.

"I don't even understand you. Why did you hide Beth if you didn't think that whatever Amelia felt for you was important?"

"Because it was mine. You know?"

"What?"

"Jesus." He threw his hands up into the air and started pacing in the parking lot. I really hoped he got hit by a car. Then that reminded me of Devin, and I realized I really needed a fucking drink.

"It's hard to be with Amelia. She has so much energy. And things needed to be done right then and there. Everything was about her. Nothing was enough. You know?"

What. The. Fuck?

Everything was about everyone else with Amelia. Yes, we all helped her with her work, but she threw herself into helping everyone else. We were the ones that offered to help her. Nobody expected to work on job sites with her. We simply showed up if we thought she needed the help. We joked that she worked us hard, but she really didn't. And she was always there for us. No matter what, she was there. She'd always been there for me, and it wasn't until recently that we truly became friends. Sure, she was in emotional upheaval at the moment—thanks to this asshole—and yes, we had all rallied around her as much as we could. Probably a little too much, hence the fake relationship.

But Jesus Christ.

"You know, I don't know. I don't know what the fuck you were thinking when it came to her. You should go. Before I kick your ass. Fuck you."

Tobey sneered. Fucking sneered. "You know what? Whatever. You should probably date her. After all, you're the slut that's used to dating tons of women. Maybe you could teach her something. Then she can get over me."

He turned on his heel and got into his car, and I just stood there, wondering who the fuck this man was in front of me. Because this was not the Tobey that I had known for so long.

This wasn't the guy that Amelia had fallen in love with.

As the man drove off, leaving me standing alone in the parking lot, I had to wonder what the hell I was going to do about Amelia.

Did I tell her about this? No, it would probably hurt her.

But I needed to do something.

And then, as if I hadn't thought about her enough, my phone rang.

I looked at the readout and pinched the bridge of my nose, trying to force myself to be calm and to slow my heart rate.

"Hey," I said, smiling.

"Hey, do you want to go to dinner tonight?" Amelia asked, her voice a little distant.

"I just got off work, and I'm starving. So, is this a fake date?" I asked, trying to sound happy and like I was teasing.

"That or just a friends date. I don't know. I'm really not good at this lying thing, and I know we're making a huge mistake. So, let's go eat dinner and pretend that everything's okay. My treat."

I smiled then and looked down at my feet, wondering if I was really baring myself like I felt. "A friends date works, Amelia."

"Good. I can come pick you up."

"Yeah, let's do that."

Then I hung up, wondering what I was going to say to her. And why just the sound of her voice warmed me inside. Because this was a bad idea.

All of it was a bad idea.

But it was sure as hell better than anything that Tobey had to offer.

At least I knew that much.

Even if it was all a mistake.

# ELEVEN

*Amelia*

"A FRIENDS DATE?"

What the fuck was a *friends date,* and why the hell had I offered to go on one with Tucker tonight? I was losing my damn mind.

No, I'd lost it when I put on that new bra and panty set —the one I'd later tossed in the trash since I never wanted to see it again.

I quickly pushed that thought out of my head and grabbed my bag so I could head out to pick up Tucker.

I figured since we were going about everything that we were doing wrong, I might as well be the one to pick *him* up, rather than him picking me up.

It had made sense in my mind at the time, but then

again, so had a lot of things recently.

I really wasn't good at this whole fake relationship thing. Not that I was good at real relationships either.

I got into my car, aware that it was getting colder outside, and grateful that I had pulled on my heavy coat with the fake fur trim instead of my regular leather one.

I probably looked as if I were ready to fight the Abominable Snowman, but at least I was warm.

I was also wearing a black top with lace that went all the way up my neck, as well as tight black pants and boots that went up to my knees.

I'd pretty much covered every inch of myself, the fact that I had done so a bit defensively notwithstanding.

Because Tucker had already seen me practically naked at this point. I didn't want to start off another evening as just friends while walking around nude. And maybe my wardrobe choices were a little bit of me wanting to be covered up for my own sake, as well. After all, I didn't want to keep showing my boobs to people when it ended badly for everyone involved.

I pulled into Tucker's driveway. He must've been watching for me, because he came out the front door immediately, locking up behind himself before zipping his coat up to his neck and jogging towards me. I didn't even have to turn off the car or get out. He was suddenly there and sliding into my passenger seat, giving me that wicked smile of his.

The one that did weird things to my insides. But I ignored it. Mostly because this was only a friend thing. He was my friend.

And, yes, if we went on a fake date, he would earn the right to kiss me again. I honestly didn't know if I wanted that. Because while it had been one of the most amazing kisses I'd ever had in my life, it didn't mean that it would be smart for either of us to continue doing it. In fact, it was probably the worst thing we could do.

"I see you found the place," Tucker said, slinking down as he put on his seatbelt.

"I've been here before. A few times."

I backed out of his driveway so we could head to the restaurant I loved. I knew Tucker liked Korean food too since I had seen him eat it. So, hopefully, he would like the place, as well.

"Well, considering this is just a friends date, I didn't know if I should start with my usual lines."

I snorted. "Your lines?"

"You know. 'Hey, did the fall hurt?'" he asked, lowering his voice.

I rolled my eyes. "If you say that I must have fallen from heaven because I'm so angelic or some shit like that, I'm going to have to kick your ass."

He smiled, shaking his head. "Well, I would've said it with a little more finesse than that. Not that I've ever actually used that line. They only use that in the movies. Or if you're really drunk at a bar."

"Good to know that you're not that pathetic."

"*That* pathetic? So, I have a little bit of patheticness in me? I don't know how I feel about that."

"I'm sure you're fine. And, really, this is just a friends date. More like dinner with a friend. We don't actually have to use the word *date*."

"I kind of like it," he said, reaching out to grip my hand and giving it a squeeze before letting it go again. I moved my hand from the gearshift where it rested and put it back on the steering wheel. Yes, space would be good. Lots and lots of space. Honestly, we probably shouldn't even be out tonight, but I really wasn't good at making smart decisions recently. Or ever for that matter. I could make good ones for work and for family, but not for myself apparently.

"So, where are we going?" he asked, leaning back in the seat. I purposely did not look at him, mostly because I really wanted to look at him.

"We're going to that new Korean place. Well, okay, it's not really new. It's been around for a couple of years. But I always call it the 'new place' because I went there on opening weekend, and now I have to go as much as possible."

"Oh, yeah. I love that place. I've been there with Devin a few times. He loves it, too."

A thick silence fell between us. I was pretty sure you

could almost reach out and touch it.

"Should I not have brought him up?" he asked, confusion in his voice.

I shook my head and flipped on my blinker to turn into the parking lot. "No. You should. It's just weird. I don't like that we're lying to him."

"I don't either."

"And I know it was my idea. I just really liked the fact that there was no pity in their eyes. And that's all on me."

"I'm the one who's going along with this."

"And I still don't know why."

"Because I don't want you to feel as if people pity you."

The way he said that, I wasn't actually sure if that was the whole truth. But then again, I didn't think either of us really knew the reasons for *anything* anymore.

Probably not the best thing. "I need to tell him."

"Okay. We will."

"I don't know when, though," I said quickly as we got out of the car.

"Yeah, that's going to be a fun conversation, but we'll get through it. Now, enough of that. It's just a friends date, right?" he said as he took my hand, giving it a squeeze as we walked into the restaurant. "That means there's nothing to worry about. No need to be nervous or feel weird. We're going to have fun, talk about stupid shit, and just be friends."

"Is that what a friends date entails?"

"Since we're making up the term, we can damn sure ensure that's what it entails. You don't have to do anything you don't want to do."

"I like going on friends dates. As long as they're with you, I guess." I couldn't believe I'd just said that. What was wrong with me?

But Tucker smiled at me, ignoring my idiocy as we went up to the hostess stand.

The woman was a brunette with wide eyes and a gorgeous smile. Her white button-up shirt and pants fit her so well, I could see every single curve she had.

"Hi there, Samantha," Tucker said after looking at the lady's nametag.

I resisted the urge to roll my eyes given where her nametag was strategically placed. Considering that her boobs were even bigger than mine, there really wasn't anywhere else to put it but right there on the swell of them.

I didn't blame her, though. She was hot. And I felt like I wasn't. But I wasn't going to let myself feel jealous. It was a friends date. Tucker was allowed to flirt with anybody he wanted. Not that he was actually flirting. He was only being nice. Because he was Tucker. Of course, from the way Samantha's eyes lit up, and she looked like a cat in cream, I had a feeling she wanted all the flirting. Well, she could have it. Because I didn't need it. Tucker and I were friends.

*Keep telling yourself that, Amelia. It's totally true.*

"Well, hi there. What can I do for you?"

Was Samantha's voice breathy? Yeah, there was a little smoke in there.

I was pretty sure she'd had a higher-pitched voice when I heard her earlier. But what did I know? Clearly, this was the Tucker effect.

"Table for two, please."

He looked over at me and then reached out to squeeze my hand, but this time, he didn't let go.

I looked down at our clasped hands and then up at him, shaking my head.

Okay, then. Weirdo.

I didn't miss the look of disappointment, and maybe even a little anger in Samantha's eyes.

Well, Tucker was hot. I couldn't blame her. I'd feel jealous too if I thought he was flirting with me. Yes, he had kissed me. But it was only a little kiss. One that was barely anything. It meant nothing.

It had to mean nothing.

"Oh. Yeah, right this way."

She took the menus, gave Tucker a long, lingering look, and then turned on her heel, expecting us to follow her.

Tucker looked at me, and I gestured after the very curvaceous and sexy Samantha.

"Well, come on. Let's go eat."

"What's that look for?" Tucker asked.

"You seriously don't know?"

"No. Enlighten me."

"Come on. We need to go sit down at our table behind Samantha, or she'll be even more disappointed." He looked confused for a moment, and I shook my head, pulling him along so we could go find our table.

I did not miss the many glances from both men and women as we made our way. Though I didn't really think any of them were for me. Sure, people hit on me, but I wasn't Tucker. There was something about him. He was beyond sexy, but it wasn't only his looks. He had this way about him that drew people in like moths to a flame. You didn't even know that you were leaning closer, putting yourself out on a limb to be nearer to him until you were there. I hadn't noticed that before, not when I thought Tobey was my one and only. I was clearly missing out there, but Tucker had only been my friend. He was still my friend —even though I knew what he looked like almost naked.

And what his mouth felt like on mine.

And I really needed to stop thinking about that. I didn't want to be all red-faced and breathy and moaning in my seat as I thought about him. That would not be good for anybody. "Thank you," I said to Samantha as she gestured toward the booth in the corner.

"You're so welcome," the woman said, looking directly at Tucker.

She set down both menus in front of him, winked, and sauntered off, her hips swaying just slightly.

"You know, this could get annoying if I didn't realize

that that's exactly how people always act around you."

"Really?" he asked, shaking his head as he handed me a menu. "And how do they act?"

"Oh, you know. The normal hitting on you thing, where they clearly can't stop themselves from wanting to bow down at your feet and ask you out."

Tucker rolled his eyes.

"It's not that bad."

"Um, yes it is."

"I see men hit on you all the time. You're beautiful. And you just have this way about you. That smile lures them in like bees to a flower."

My stomach tumbled at those words, my cheeks going hot. "It's not the same. People love being near you."

He shrugged and leaned back in the booth. "Maybe. But I think it's the same with you. You were just hyper-focused on someone before so you didn't see it."

I opened my mouth to say something, but he reached out and ran his knuckle over my hand before resting his palm over my fingers. "Forget I said that. We're not going to talk about him. Ever."

There was a growl to his tone this time that kind of worried me, but I didn't know where it came from. It was even worse than usual. Had something happened? I didn't really think the two of them ran in the same circles outside of when they were with the Carr group, but I didn't know. Maybe I was seeing something that wasn't there.

"There are at least six women in this restaurant right now, and probably a couple of men, eyeing you."

He snorted. "There's probably the same amount looking at you. Men and women."

"Probably because I'm next to you. You've always been a ladies' man."

He frowned a bit, looking down at his menu. We didn't have time to finish that line of conversation though, because the waiter was suddenly there, handing over two glasses of water and taking our drink orders. We both ordered Japanese beer since it was a fusion place, not just Korean, and then leaned back, our menus closed. Apparently, we both knew what we wanted to order. That was good. Because I was starving.

"You are a ladies' man," I said again, wanting to finish the conversation.

"But I don't cheat. I don't poach. I have rules. I'm not an asshole."

He looked so annoyed at that, that I reached across the booth and ran my fingers down his arm. He smiled, flipping his palm over so I could put my hand on his. Friends did that, right?

"You're not an asshole. And I know you never lead women on. It's just that I know you go on a lot of dates."

Tucker shrugged. "I go on a lot of first and second dates. I don't want to get married."

I don't know why that was a little disappointing to hear,

but I'd already known that. "Because of what happened with your parents?"

"Maybe. Yeah. I don't want the whole commitment thing and making a new family. It made a lot more sense when I was younger, and I put that label on myself. Now, I guess it's habit for me. I like my life. I like the family I've made. I like my friends. I don't need anything more."

I didn't have time to delve into that or think about exactly what he meant because I looked behind him, and my eyes went wide. I swallowed hard, and Tucker frowned, turning around so he could see what I was looking at.

"Ah, well, we knew he liked the place."

Erin and Devin waved from their table. Erin smiled widely, while my brother only smiled a little. He didn't look too angry, though. He looked resigned. And maybe a little...hopeful?

My stomach clenched, and I suddenly wasn't hungry for dinner anymore.

"I guess this is a fake date again," Tucker said, disappointment in his tone. It seemed we weren't very good at this thing.

"Yeah. Sorry about that."

He scooted over in the booth, put his arm around my shoulder, and then kissed my temple. "It's fine. We'll just do what we were. Nothing needs to change."

I looked up at him then and nodded, trying to smile. "Yeah. Nothing needs to change."

But I had a feeling everything was going to shift. And I really wasn't good at change.

We finished our dinner, Devin and Erin giving us space and not coming over to say hi. They were on a date as well, so I didn't feel too bad about that. They wanted space for themselves, considering they worked far too hard and rarely had time for each other beyond stolen moments. I had a feeling that Devin didn't really know what to do about Tucker and me, just like we didn't know what to do about him, so we gave each other space. But it wasn't a real date anyway. It was a fake one.

And why did I hate that so much?

"Okay, that was one fake date on the table," Tucker said as we headed down the path to his house. I was dropping him off, but I wanted to walk him to his door. After all, I had been the one to pick him up. I might as well continue the weird night.

"Yeah. Sorry about that. I really just wanted us to be two friends at dinner."

He frowned, turning in front of me to cup my face. "We were two friends at dinner. No matter what labels we put on each other or this thing we're doing, regardless of what happens next, we were two friends then, and we're two friends now. That's not going to change, Amelia. I hope you get that."

There was such intensity in his gaze and in his words that I froze, my mouth going dry.

"I don't want it to change," I whispered. "I like what we are."

But the thing was, we'd already changed things. We were different than the people we'd been before I made this arrangement. And before Tucker started coming over to make sure I was okay. Everything was different. And while I didn't particularly like change, I kind of liked this. I wanted more of it. And that scared me.

Before I could think about that more, though, before I could run away or try to forget all of it, Tucker was looking into my eyes, and I could hardly breathe.

"I think you owe me a payment," he said, his voice a low growl.

"Oh, I guess I do," I whispered, my voice breathy. My thighs clenched, and my stomach turned, but I looked up at him, and I couldn't help but want more.

And when his lips were on mine, his hands still on my face, I wrapped my arms around his waist and pulled him closer.

He groaned into my mouth, tasting a little like beer, a bit of sweetness from the meal, and a whole lot like Tucker.

He kissed me, and I wanted more.

For someone who made mistake after mistake, that should worry me.

But with Tucker's heat next to me, his mouth on mine, I really couldn't care less.

# TWELVE

*Tucker*

I KNEW I SHOULD MOVE AWAY.

Once again, I knew I wouldn't.

I finally had to pull back to catch my breath.

And when I did, I rested my forehead against hers. Her grip on my hips tightened, and I held back a smile. This was wrong. This would get us into so much trouble. But I couldn't help it. Amelia was my weakness. My temptation. And I hadn't even realized it.

How had she done this to me?

How had I let myself get involved in this?

But then I couldn't really think anymore. I couldn't care.

Because I had her in my arms. And I needed more. Wanted more.

"What are we doing?" she whispered, her voice coming out in sharp pants.

My breaths matched hers, and I just sighed, my hands running down her back to cover her ass. We were outside my house, in full view of anyone who wanted to look. But it was late and dark enough that no one could really see us. I hadn't left the porch light on, and the chill in the air was biting enough that no one would be outside to pay any attention to us.

It was just Amelia and me. And we could be the ones that sent us down the path of our own turmoil. Nobody else.

"I don't know," I said, finally answering her. "But I don't think I want to stop."

She looked up at me then, her lips swollen from my kisses, kind of begging for more. At least that's what I thought. What I hoped.

"Maybe we should go inside."

My dick stood at attention, pressing hard into the zipper of my pants. Figured. "Oh?" There was so much in that single word, that one sound escaping on a growl, that I was afraid both of us were going to rip off the other's clothes right then and there. Not that we would.

"To talk," she said again, her voice equally breathy. I couldn't get my heart to stop racing, not with the way she was looking at me, and I had a feeling she had the same problem.

What the hell was wrong with us?

"To talk," I repeated, not knowing if that was the truth or not.

I swallowed hard and then let her go, only to grab her hand with my left one and use my right one to get into the house. I closed the door firmly behind us, and then I was on her again, absorbing her taste. Talking would have to wait.

Her back was pressed against the door, my hands on her face as I deepened the kiss, our tongues tangling. She moaned into my mouth, her hands moving down my back, her fingernails pricking my skin even through my jacket.

I wanted to rip off that fur thing she wore, the one that wasn't really fur but made her look adorable.

I wanted to strip her out of all her clothes and lick her slowly from head to toe. Every inch of her. I wanted to spread her legs and slam into her, feeling that sense of peace I hadn't known I wanted.

I wanted to feel her wet heat, feel her cunt clamp around me as I came inside her, and she screamed my name.

I wanted my lips on those tantalizing breasts I had seen once already. I wanted to squeeze and mold and bite.

I wanted her on her knees as I gripped her hair, sliding in and out of that luscious mouth of hers. I wanted those lips even more swollen, her tongue coated with my come as she swallowed me whole.

I wanted my head between her thighs, licking up her sweet juices as I gently bit down on her clit, using my fingers to bring her to ecstasy.

I wanted to reach around and play with her ass, see if she liked that, discover if she would let my fingers explore.

I wanted all of that.

And it made me a fucking bastard.

But I really didn't care.

Because all I wanted was her. Even if it sent us both to hell.

"Tell me to stop," I said, pulling away from her. We were still touching, our bodies pressed against one another. But I'd put both hands above her head on the door, trying not to let my hand slide down her body. She groaned, arching her hips away from the door and into mine.

I froze, trying to count to ten so my cock wouldn't explode right then and there.

She was sin and temptation and everything that I knew I shouldn't have, but I didn't care. I wanted her then and there. Even if it broke us both.

"I don't know if I can tell you to stop," she whispered. "What are we doing?" she asked again.

I swallowed hard, closing my eyes and trying to count again.

"We can call this...friend sex. Beard sex. No ties, no commitments. We just stay who we are. Friends first. Lovers second."

Her eyes widened at my use of the word *lovers*, but I hoped it was okay. I didn't want to lose her. But I had to have her. Selfish, that's what I was.

But with my cock so hard, and my heart beating so fast, I didn't give a shit.

"Beard sex. We can do that." She grinned then, her hands running through the softness of my actual beard. "And you already have the accoutrements."

"I cannot believe you used the word *accoutrements* right now. I'm thinking in grunts." I erotically rotated my hips, and her eyes widened, her pupils getting large.

"Oh, that's good. No more words."

I shook my head, gritting my teeth. "A few more."

"Okay. Anything."

"Friends first. That's what we are. It's just you. Me. For as long as this lasts."

I didn't cheat. I didn't poach. I didn't do any of that shit, but some thought I did. I might go out with lots of women, but I wasn't the bastard that some thought I was.

"Deal. Just you and me. No waitresses or ladies you meet at the grocery store."

I grinned at that, then bent down and bit her lip. I licked away the sting, and her eyes widened.

"I can do that. You and me. But that means no more random guys offering to help you lift shit and then checking you out."

She shook her head, laughter in her eyes even with the lust. "It's not like that. I can do my own lifting."

"Yeah. You can. And I'll be there to help you, too. But no more other friend sex. No more other beard sex. We're the only two that get to have that."

"I'm pretty sure we're the only two that will ever call it 'beard sex.' Ever. In the history of civilization."

"Well, then I guess it's special for us."

"Special." She paused, her throat working as she swallowed hard. "I like special."

"Good." And then my lips were on hers again, and I tried to keep counting so I wouldn't come.

Her hands slid down my back, cupping my ass, and I grinned against her mouth, rocking my hips into her. She moaned each time I made contact, and I couldn't wait to slide into her.

She licked her lips as I moved away, but I kissed her again before reaching behind her back so I could slide my hands down and grip her ass. I gave it a hard squeeze, rocking my hips into her, and she groaned.

"I'm going to lick every inch of you, then I'm going to make you come on my mouth, and then on my cock. And if you let me, I'm going to play with this little ass of yours right here and see exactly how hard you can come." I slid my fingers along the seam of her crack through her pants as I said it, and her eyes widened, her mouth parting.

"You want to play with my ass?" she asked, incredulousness in her voice.

"If you let me. A finger or two."

She snorted. "How about just one. Maybe we can add a second later."

I froze, and so did she. I had a feeling she hadn't thought she'd answer like that.

"Are you serious?"

"Yeah. I've used a plug or two in my time. I think I can deal with your finger."

I let my head fall back as I closed my eyes and groaned.

"You really shouldn't say things like that when I'm already so far on edge. I may not even get inside you before I come at this point."

She laughed, reaching between us to grip my cock. My head shot back so I could look at her, and I groaned. "Don't do that, baby."

"You mean...this?" She so innocently asked before stroking me through my jeans, giving the base a squeeze.

I leaned away from her touch, and when she tried to reach for me, I took both hands in one of mine and put them above her head against the door. "Okay, my turn."

"Show me what you got, Tucker."

"Gladly." Then I kissed her again, leaving soft bites and nibbles along her jaw and down her neck. I let her hands go so I could strip her out of her jacket and then tug her shirt over her head. That left her in her bra and pants and boots, and I swallowed hard, trying to look my fill.

I let my jacket fall to the floor, toed off my shoes so I wouldn't forget later, and then moved down her chest to leave smacking kisses along with tops of her breasts over her bra.

"Like the lace," I said, cupping her bra-covered breasts and letting my thumb slide against her nipple.

She sucked in little sharp breaths and nodded.

"I'm glad you like it. Although I wore it for me, not you."

"Well, I like the way you treat yourself."

Then I leaned down and sucked her nipple through the lace, loving the way she purred.

I gave the same attention to her other peak, grinning as I pulled back before kissing her on her lips again.

Her hand slid up and down my back, tugging at my shirt, so I reached around and pulled it over my head, leaving me shirtless and loving the way her gaze raked over me.

"You know I saw you in that towel earlier, but damn, your body's a little intimidating."

I raised a brow and looked down at her curves. "Um, hello, have you seen yourself in a mirror? Fucking sexy as hell. Never feel intimidated by me."

"You're sheer perfection, Tucker. And you know it."

I shrugged, pushing back some memories from before. I

hadn't always looked like this. I worked hard now because I had the time and the money. I hadn't had either when I was younger, and I had been rail-thin. It was hard to stay fit and healthy when you were going from foster home to foster home. And, sometimes, they didn't have enough food, even though they got money from the state.

Fingertips feathered along my cheek, and I looked down at her.

"I didn't mean to make you go away." Her voice went soft and straight to my heart. I swallowed hard.

"No worries. I'm right here. Just you and me."

Her gaze searched my face, and she smiled. "Good."

I kissed her again, this time a little slower before my mind was entirely back into it, and then I deepened it. I wanted to go hard, fast, and pour out my demons. Be ourselves. If we went too soft, got too romantic, it would only hurt us in the end. This would just be beard sex, whatever the fuck that was. Hard, fast, and everything we needed.

At least, I hoped so.

I undid her bra, let it fall to the floor, then I lavished attention on her breasts, looking at the red tips of her nipples as I sucked hard.

She moaned, her body shaking. I didn't know if I wanted her to get off at the door.

But I wanted her, and I wasn't sure I could wait.

"I want to fuck you against this door. You going to let me?"

"You sure are taking your time about it," she teased.

I gave her a hard, smacking kiss, and reached around to my side table where I'd left a condom—not because I'd thought I would ever have sex here, but because I'd pulled them out of my wallet earlier.

She raised a brow, and I blushed.

"I had them in my wallet earlier, but I didn't want to bring them for our date and make you feel weird. So, I left them here. Good idea, though."

She just snorted and nodded. "Well, you might as well put them to good use."

I kissed her again and then kept touching her.

Our hands roamed over each other. As she undid my belt and the fastenings of my pants, they fell to the floor.

I quickly pushed down my boxer briefs, letting them fall as well. Her eyes widened.

"What?" I asked, laughing.

"I would say I'm afraid you're not going to fit, but I don't want to go straight porn movie."

"Hey, we quote porn. We'd be good at it. Damn good at it."

And then I went to my knees and undid her pants.

She groaned as I kissed her over her panties and then tugged her pants over her ass and down to her knees.

She tried to kick off her boots, but I wouldn't let her.

"No, I'm going to fuck you like this. With your legs pressed together, and your ass looking all plump and ready for me."

"Really?"

"Really."

I kissed her again before flipping her around so her breasts were pressed against the door.

I nipped and nibbled her ass, spreading her cheeks before biting some more.

I licked along the base of her spine and then looked up at her neck before biting down on the curve where it met her shoulder.

"Tucker," she whispered, and then I grinned.

I slid the condom over my length before rubbing my cock along the seam of her ass.

She stiffened and then looked over her shoulder at me, her brow raised.

"Um, excuse me. I'm not quite sure I said yes to all of that."

I just smiled before kissing her cheek.

"I'll be gentle. I promise."

I slid my hand between her and the door and cupped her heat.

"Tucker," she whispered.

I just kept kissing down her neck, along her shoulder, rocking along the seam of her ass as I played with her clit and the folds of her pussy.

"You're already wet for me."

"I think I've been wet for you since dinner."

I groaned, my hand digging into her hip as my other continued playing with her.

"I need you inside of me," she whispered, wiggling against me.

My hand tightened on her hip as I slowly worked my way inside of her with my fingers. "Not until you come on my hand first."

"Tucker," she panted.

But I didn't stop. I just kept playing, needing.

I moved quickly, my thumb stroking her clit. Suddenly, she called out my name, her cunt clamping around my fingers.

I kept moving, her flesh swollen and wet. And when she stopped shaking, I slid my fingers out of her and grinned, moving my hand around so I could put one of my wet fingers against her lips.

"Taste."

Her eyes widened, and her tongue reached out, licking her wetness from her lip.

"Good girl."

And then I reached down to my cock, slid her wetness over my condom-covered dick and slowly teased her entrance from behind.

"Tucker," she whispered again.

And then I slammed home.

We both froze, the shock of her tight heat gripping my cock almost too much.

She was so tight, so wet, and my eyes crossed. It was hard to keep from coming right then, but I held myself back, both of us looking at each other as she acclimated to my dick.

"Jesus Christ," I whispered, and she grinned at me.

"Get moving, boy, or I'm going to start moving for you."

She arched her back, and I went a little deeper. We both moaned.

"Got that. Yeah, I can do that."

And then I moved.

I slid in and out of her, holding her hip with one hand while using my other to press her shoulders to the door.

Her pants were still around her thighs, her boots up to her knees, and it made her pliant to my touch.

Which had to be the hottest thing I'd ever seen.

I moved my hand from her shoulder, and the other from her hip so I could spread her cheeks as I slid in and out of her.

I looked down at her ass where I spread her and grinned before reaching around to gather some of her juices to wet my fingers again.

"Tucker, I didn't realize you were such an ass man."

I pumped hard again, sending a shock through both of us. She closed her eyes, moaning.

"I'm a tit man. An ass man. And for now, I'm your man."

She froze just for a moment, barely even noticeable, but I saw it.

I'd have to be careful.

We'd both have to be careful.

I slowly teased her back entrance, but I didn't firmly insert my finger. I didn't have any lube on me, and I didn't want to hurt her.

I was already afraid we would both end up hurt at the end of this as it was.

But I pushed those thoughts from my mind and continued pushing in and pulling out of her, fucking her hard as we both panted, our bodies sweat-slick.

As my balls tightened, the base of my spine tingling, I reached around and flicked my fingers over her clit.

She arched her back, coming on my cock, squeezing me hard as I came with her.

I shook, keeping my hips pumping as I wrung out both of our orgasms, but I couldn't stop. I needed more.

So I pulled out of her fully, even as she reached for me. I picked her up and cradled her to my chest.

"What are you doing?"

"I'm not done yet," I growled out.

Her eyes widened, and then she bounced on my plush couch as I threw her on it.

"Are you serious?" she said with a laugh. And then she wasn't laughing.

I had her boots off, her pants thrown over my shoulder, and my head between her legs.

I lapped up her juices, eating her out as she screamed my name, her hands tugging at my hair.

I slid one finger inside her, and then two more, fucking her hard with my fingers as I kissed and bit and sucked on her clit.

She wriggled under my hold, and I kept going. As she came again, and then was about to come for the fourth time, I pulled away. She moaned.

I reached for the second condom I'd pulled out, ripped off the old one, made sure to put it on a tissue, pulled on the new one, and slammed into her.

Her eyes widened, and I grinned.

"Again? How?"

"Apparently, you worked your magic quite well, temptress."

And then I moved. We kept kissing, our hands running over each other as I slammed into her on the couch, her legs wrapped around my waist, and my mouth all over her body. Any place I could reach.

She was doing the same to me, and I was afraid we would burn out, the heat between us too much.

When I came again, her body clamped around me, her own orgasm a little softer this time as if she had nothing left.

But it didn't matter.

This was all there was, all there could be.

And as I held her close, I knew we had made a terrible mistake.

I couldn't look her in the eyes. Instead, I just held her, our bodies still pressed together, my softening cock still deep inside of her.

This had been possibly the best moment of my entire life.

And I knew we should never do it again.

Even though we probably would.

And every time we did, we'd likely ruin a little more of what we had.

We'd ruin it all.

# Thirteen

*Amelia*

As mistakes went, the night before had been a doozy.

But I was too sore and sated to care at the moment.

I hadn't slept over at Tucker's, though part of me had wanted to. After we'd gone one more round, I'd somehow found my clothes and the strength to leave the house. He hadn't stopped me, hadn't asked me to stay.

And though I should have been hurt by that, I was actually grateful.

Because I couldn't have stayed.

And yet there had been something in his eyes telling me I could have if I'd wanted to.

We were both going down a path we shouldn't, one that

was far more reckless than anything we could have done, but I didn't think either of us was going to turn back now.

At least, not yet.

Tucker was coming over later for dinner, something that worried me but also didn't. Because friends did that, right? They had fun as friends, and they ate food together. Just because he was coming over to my house after he'd made me come multiple times the night before at his place didn't mean anything had to be weird.

And considering that I'd never thought that sentence before in my life, I figured I had reached a new low in my weirdness.

Tucker didn't do commitment. And I was still getting over Tobey. There was no room for a relationship.

It had to remain what we were now. Friends.

With benefits.

Because that had to be what we were now. Right?

I shook my head and then went to water my plants.

I tried to keep a few indoor plants in the house, though I was better at keeping them alive outside. I might be a landscape architect, but sometimes, houseplants and I just did not get along.

I'd already worked that morning on countless invoices and creating plans for when the ground thawed, and spring came.

Looking at my proposed list, I was going to be busy, and would finally be able to hire someone full-time, rather than just part-time. I had someone in mind, and we'd been talking about it for a while, but I didn't know if Jamie would agree. If not, Iman might join me. She was new at this line of work and was still in school, but she had taken some time off to find herself. Since I was in the process of finding myself, too, I figured it was kind of the perfect plan.

Jamie had been working for me longer and was already on the path to becoming a full-time employee. I didn't know if Iman would be ready or not.

Time would tell. And maybe, just maybe, I would be able to hire two full-time people.

I shook my head. No, I wasn't there yet. I was getting there, though. My business was prospering. And while I worked far too hard, I liked the work. I loved what I did.

I enjoyed making people happy and plants even happier.

I liked someone being able to go outside into their back yard to relax in their very own oasis. I took pride in having people walk into their homes after walking through a wonderful yard that was welcoming and easy to maintain.

At least, I tried for the easy-to-maintain part. Sometimes, things got a little out of control, but it wasn't my fault. People wanted what they wanted, and while I tried to talk them out of it at times, I also had to listen to the customer.

I shook my head and put away my watering can right as the doorbell rang. I frowned, wondering if Tucker was early. But that couldn't be. He'd said he had a long shift today, which is why we hadn't spent the night together. He wouldn't have been able to get a lot of sleep, and neither would I.

But that was fine, I hadn't needed to stay with him overnight.

It wouldn't have been safe for either of us.

I looked through the peephole and frowned, not recognizing the woman on the other side. I opened the door and smiled, even though I really wasn't in the mood for a solicitor. Nobody ever actually heeded those signs. I really should get one of those doorbells with a video camera or something so I could just talk from my house or my phone from work.

"Hi, can I help you?"

"You need to stay away from him." She glared.

I blinked, looking over at the woman. I honestly had no idea who she was, but she sure as hell knew me.

She had dark brown hair and wore it in waves hanging over her shoulders and down her back. Her eyes were done up in cat-eye precision, perfect makeup and eyeliner I was kind of jealous about.

She had even contoured her face, something I'd tried and still couldn't do. Zoey would have to teach me.

The woman had on a lacy turtleneck and a leather jacket, even though it was a little too cold for just that. Her pants looked painted on, and her boots had to have five-inch stiletto heels.

She looked amazing and sexy.

But she sure as hell wasn't smiling.

"I'm sorry, you have me at a disadvantage. Who are you?"

"Oh, you know who I am."

"I really don't."

Was this one of Tucker's women? Dear God, how had she found me? A weight settled in my gut, and I rubbed my stomach. I really didn't want to get in the way of whatever Tucker had going with this woman. He had said he was single, and that we shouldn't be with anyone else while together. But given the way this woman was glaring at me, apparently, that wasn't the case.

"I'm Beth, you bitch."

My eyes widened, and I took an involuntary step back, my hand on the edge of my door. She leaned forward.

I just blinked at her, trying to comprehend exactly what was going on. This was Tobey's Beth. His other half. The one that he'd said was his everything.

And she was here. Calling *me* a bitch.

What the hell?

As I looked at her again, I saw the similarities between us, and something slid over me. We had the same color hair, the same shape. She was probably a size smaller, but she looked like she worked out. I did not work out as much as I should, but I was happy with my size. We had similar cheekbones, but different eyes, and she was way better at makeup and styling than I was.

She looked like someone who could have been my friend, someone I'd want to ask for help in figuring out what to wear for a date, or how to do those wings at the edges of her eyelids.

I thought all of that in a bare instant as I studied her, wondering why the person I had thought was my best friend forever would want her.

And not even want her over me.

That ship had sailed.

But I didn't like the vehemence in her tone. I didn't like how she made me feel.

"Beth. Tobey's Beth," I said.

"Oh, now you know who I am. Stay away from him. You weren't good for him. I'm his girlfriend. I am going to marry him one day. You need to back off. Every time you call him or get close to him, you just confuse him and make things difficult. And how dare you come onto him like you did? He said no, and you wouldn't take that as an answer."

My eyebrows went up on my forehead, and I glared. "Excuse me? No. That's not how it happened."

"He told me exactly how it happened. Now you're going to call him a liar? Just because you aren't good enough for him, doesn't mean you can come around and try to ruin our relationship. I love him, and he loves me. And you're always in the way. Just leave him alone."

"What the fuck?" I whispered to myself, and she just narrowed her eyes at me. "Leave us alone."

"You need to leave," I said, my voice far calmer than I felt. This woman, this Beth, was so emotional. She had to be scared of losing whatever she had with Tobey to the point that she was lashing out. Because I would like to think that Tobey wouldn't fall in love with someone who could say these things.

But maybe he had told her a different story. Or perhaps what I did had been far worse than I thought.

"Stay away from him."

"No problem. You don't have to worry about that."

Because I didn't think I'd talk with Tobey again. At least not in person for a long while. Everything was out of control, and I didn't know why things hurt so badly.

She stomped away and got into her sedan before peeling out of my driveway and driving off.

I shook in my doorway for a bit and then closed the door before I let all the heat out.

I slowly made my way to my phone, my hands shaking.

**Me:** *Stay away, Tobey. Please. Beth was here. I don't know what you said to her. But you just need to stay away.*

I sank down to the floor, my hands shaking as I looked at my phone and watched those three little dots pop up as Tobey responded.

**Tobey:** *I'm sorry that she came there. I didn't think she would. But you need to stay away from Beth too. That would be best for all of us.*

He wanted *me* to stay away. And all I'd done was tell

him that I loved him. Now, everything had changed. Who was this person? This wasn't the guy I had fallen for.

Maybe I hadn't really loved him at all if this was how things turned out. Maybe I just thought I had. Because this wasn't even the same person who had been my best friend for as long as I could remember.

The Tobey I knew would never treat me like this.

Maybe he'd always been this way, and I just hadn't seen it, or maybe Beth had done this to him. Regardless, I would never blame someone else's choices on another. If he was acting like this, then that was on him. Nobody was forcing him to be this way.

I didn't even know Beth.

Apparently, I didn't know Tobey either.

I put my phone into the drawer next to me and slowly stood up, my knees shaking.

I was trying to figure out exactly who I was without him in my life, and now it seemed it wouldn't just be temporary. I would never be able to call him again to see how he was doing. To see if he wanted to watch a movie or check out the latest *Star Trek* convention down the road. We would never be able to hit up 16th Street Mall and get coffee or see who was playing at the local bar.

We would never play video games and try to see who could hit each other the most with shells as we played *Mario Kart* like we were kids.

Though I didn't think I'd ever want to do any of that again anyway.

Even though I had told him that I loved him, I hadn't crossed the line into menace. I hadn't been cruel about it.

And now Tobey made me feel like I was nothing. And every time I had contact with him again, it got worse.

He made me feel like I was worthless. That I shouldn't be with him.

And now there was Beth.

I'd never wanted to be the other woman, and she clearly wasn't the other woman in this scenario.

But now I had lost my best friend, and that hurt even more than the thought of losing the idea of the love of my life.

The doorbell rang, and I clenched my fists, hoping it wasn't Beth again or Tobey.

I didn't know what I would do if I saw Tobey again. Because I was just so angry and sad and everything else all at once.

It was like I didn't even know myself now, let alone him.

How wrong had I been? How many more mistakes could I make?

I opened the door without bothering to look through the peephole and sagged in relief as I saw Tucker.

"What's wrong, baby?" he asked as he walked right in and cupped my face. I closed the door behind him and just leaned into him. "Nothing's wrong."

"Okay, you're going to tell me exactly what's going on," he said as he pulled away from me slightly before leading me to the couch.

"Whose ass am I going to have to kick? Is it your brother's?"

I looked at him then and just shook my head.

"Really? You would kick my brother's ass?"

"I would try to," he said, holding up a finger. "I mean, don't get me wrong, I work out."

He flexed his biceps and waggled his brows. I smiled and felt far more lighthearted than I'd thought I could that afternoon.

"Oh, I know you do."

"Down, tiger. We have things to do first."

"First?"

"Yes, but...do not get me off-topic. We are going to figure out exactly what is going on with you."

I sighed, shaking my head. "It wasn't my brothers. Even though you might be able to kick their asses."

"You know I can't. Dimitri is all tatted up, and teacher or not, he could take me out with a pinky. Devin's even worse. And don't get me started on Caleb. Dear God. How do you have three big bruisers for brothers? And you're so tiny."

"I'm not tiny." I flexed my arm, and he reached out and pinched it.

"Hey," I said, rubbing the spot.

CARRIE ANN RYAN

"You're so cute."

"Okay, so it won't be my brothers kicking your ass. It'll be me."

"We both know I can pin you down."

My belly went warm, and I bit my lip.

"Excuse me. I let myself be pinned, thank you very much."

He reached out and bit my lip himself before licking away the sting. I groaned.

"You say that, yet I think we both know that isn't the case. Now, stop using sex to distract me."

"It's surprisingly easy with you."

"It's like we've been doing this all along, isn't it?" he asked with a wink, and I just shook my head before pushing him back.

"I'm fine. Really. It's just that...well, Beth was here."

He scrunched his brows. "Do I know a Beth?"

"Funny story. So, I thought it was a woman here looking for you."

This time, his brows shot straight up. "Excuse me? Why would a woman be looking for me?"

"I don't know. She just told me to stay away from *him*. And at first, I had no idea who *he* was. So, I thought it was about you."

"I'm not currently seeing anyone but you. And I'm not technically *seeing* you either because we love our shady labels."

"Hey, Shady Labels should be our band name."

He just rolled his eyes before giving me a kiss. I settled just a bit at his touch, knowing for this moment, what we were doing, was worth it. He was really good at calming me. Even though I wasn't sure exactly what any of it meant.

"Okay. Tell Uncle Tucker exactly what's going on."

"Ew, I'm totally not calling you Uncle Tucker."

He visibly shuddered, and I laughed. "Yeah, as soon as I said it, I went to that creepy place. Okay, let's backtrack, Shady Label."

"Do not use that as a nickname. It's a band name."

"Anything you say. Now, Beth? Not one of mine. I have not seen a Beth in a very long time."

"Well, I figured that out when she said her name was Beth. She's Tobey's girlfriend."

This time, his eyes went dark, a little growl escaping his throat. "What did she want?"

"Other than to call me names and tell me to stay away? I'm not sure. She was just so angry. I don't know what he's told her, but it clearly hasn't been good things. And I almost feel sorry for her."

He sighed before getting up and starting to pace. "You always think the best of people. It has to be someone who needs help. Or someone you need to feel sorry for. But you're the one who had someone come to your home and call you names. Did she hurt you? Threaten you?"

I shook my head. "No. She just said to stay away. I don't

remember exactly what else was said, but I got the gist of it. And then I texted Tobey and told him to stay away since Beth was here and it got weird. And then he said I needed to stay away from Beth."

"Are you fucking kidding me?"

"Nope. It doesn't make any sense."

"Well, I hate him. He's lucky I didn't kick his ass in that parking lot," he said quickly and then slammed his lips together.

This time I stood up and glared. "What parking lot?"

"I saw him in the parking lot of the grocery store, but I didn't hit him. We were just leaving, so I approached, and he was an asshole. Said something stupid. I almost hit him, but I didn't."

"What did he say?" I asked, my body chilled.

Tucker shook his head and then came up to me, holding me close. I didn't lean into him, though. I was suddenly worried.

"He said it was hard to be with you. That you had so much energy that it was hard to keep up or some shit like that. He was just talking out of his ass. An insecure little prick. I didn't want to lie to you, and I don't want to hurt you. So, ignore his words. I'm here. And that's all that matters." He kissed the tip of my nose as he said that, and I nodded, giving him a very fake smile. I knew he knew it wasn't real, but there really wasn't much I could do about that.

Because my former best friend couldn't be near me. And he didn't want to be. Because I was just too much. I was needy.

And look at me now, doing the same thing with Tucker.

I was making him lie to his best friend.

All because I didn't know how to handle my feelings.

Tucker's lips were on me then, his hands on my ass, holding me close to him. I pushed away, trying to suck in a breath.

"What was that?"

"Stop blaming yourself. You are not whatever the fuck he said, or what Beth said. Everybody loves being around you. And you are always there for us. You're allowed to need help once in a while. And we both know that I'm not here right now because you need me. I'm here because I want to be. So, fuck him. Okay?"

I just stood there, trying to nod as his words slid over me.

Everything was happening so fast, and yet not fast enough. Because I was trying to think about Tobey, wondering exactly what I had done wrong, but all I could do was look at the man in front of me.

All I could do was think about his words. And what he meant.

"I'm sorry," he whispered. Kissing me again.

I wrapped my arms around him and nestled against his

chest. "I'm sorry, too." I paused, my voice low. "I hate that he's done this."

"At least you didn't blame yourself that time." He rubbed his hand down my back.

"I just want things to go back to normal."

"Amelia?"

"Yeah?"

"This might be your new normal. So, I guess you're going to have to figure that out, too."

"I guess so."

"But you're not alone. You've got your family. You've got your friends. And you've got me."

I didn't ask him to promise. Didn't ask him to tell me he was sure. Because, honestly, I was afraid he wouldn't be able to guarantee that. And after thinking that I'd had that promise with Tobey for years and finding out that everything had been a lie, I really didn't want to hear another pledge like that.

So I pushed those thoughts from my head and just leaned into Tucker's hold.

I didn't know what was going to happen next. I didn't know what I was supposed to feel. But for now, I was going to pretend that everything was okay. Because, honestly, it had to be.

And in Tucker's arms, I thought maybe that could be the truth.

# Fourteen

*Amelia*

"SO, ARE YOU GOING TO TELL ME WHAT YOU'RE hiding?" Zoey asked as she helped me work in the greenhouse in my backyard.

I had put one in a year before thanks to city permits. It wasn't a large one, but it was big enough that I could work on my plants when I was at home, even in the dead of winter.

It was my happy place. My safe spot.

But, as my best friend glared at me, I had a feeling it wasn't going to be safe for long.

"What do you mean?"

Zoey just narrowed her eyes.

"Okay. You are going to have to tell me exactly what's

going on in that mind of yours. Because I know you're hiding something. And it's grating on you. Is it Tobey? Tucker? You guys seem so good right now. But then again, I thought you were doing okay with Tobey, so what do I know?"

I winced, shaking my head.

Erin sat in the corner, not speaking, but looking at both of us as we talked.

I'd brought them over to have an afternoon off, but they had wanted to work in my greenhouse. Now, I regretted it.

Because I knew I needed to be truthful.

But I didn't know where to start.

"Was it really the same with Tobey, though?" Erin asked, bringing me out of my reverie.

I frowned.

"What do you mean by that?"

"We all thought you had something with Tobey, but it was as if you were waiting. Like something wasn't truly there," Erin continued.

"You know, she's right. You're happier with Tucker. At least there's no *will they, won't they*. You guys just are. And I know you slept together. I can see it on your face," Zoey said, pointing at me.

I rubbed at my cheek, wincing.

"You can tell?"

"Well, it's not like you actually have it on your face," Erin said. Zoey and I both froze, looking over at her.

"Did you just make a semen joke?" I asked, shaking my head.

"Not a very good one. I really hope it's not on your face. I mean...shower much?"

I winced, shaking my head even as I held back laughter.

"Okay, yes, Tucker and I had sex. There. Don't tell my brother."

Erin held up her hands, looking completely innocent.

"I am not going to tell your brother that you had sex with his best friend. I'm pretty sure he already knows, though."

My eyes widened. "He can't know. He hasn't seen Tucker yet."

I'd made sure of that. Because the two of us needed to come clean to my brother as soon as we saw him next. There would be no more lying, no more making Tucker feel like a horrible person. I was still a horrible person, but Tucker did not deserve that. So, we planned to tell my brother. Not that we knew exactly what to say or what we were to each other. But shady label totally worked for us. We didn't have to know exactly who we were with one another, as long as everyone else knew that what we were was our business.

I had actually gone through and tried to write out exactly what I was going to say a few times but came up with nothing.

"Okay, let's go back to what we were talking about," I said quickly.

Erin frowned. "Okay, what were we talking about?"

"You can't get out of it that quickly," Zoey said, exasperated. "Tell us what's on your mind. Did Beth come back again?"

I'd told them about what had happened with Beth and then Tobey when they first showed up, and none of us could really figure out what to say about it. "You mean in the ten seconds that you've been here?" I asked, snorting.

"I should have said is there anything *else* to do with Beth and Tobey. I cannot believe she showed up like that."

"As someone who's almost been the other woman, or the original woman, I can understand being all territorial. It's just that I don't quite understand where she's coming from," Erin said, frowning.

"The difference is that your husband was actually cheating on you," I snapped and then went still. "Sorry. I didn't mean it like that."

"Oh. He was totally cheating on me. And that's fine. He and that woman are going to be happily married or doing whatever they want. And that's fine with me, too. I'm much happier now. As for Beth? It sounds like she's intimidated by you. Hell, I would be intimidated by you."

"Ouch." I rubbed my chest over my heart, and she just smiled at me.

"That's not what I meant. I know Tobey told Tucker something stupid in the parking lot, but what I said had nothing to do with that. All I mean is that, on the outside, you and Tobey had this amazing connection, and that could intimidate anyone. Maybe she saw that and reacted poorly because of it."

"That doesn't justify her behavior or the way Tobey's acting."

"You're right," I said, and both of them looked at me, wide-eyed. "What?"

"We just expected you to defend him again," Zoey said. "You always defend him."

"Maybe. But I'm tired of that. Yes, I probably should have gone another way with telling him how I felt, but he didn't have to lash out like he did. And he's welcome to his feelings, but he's been treating me weirdly, and he completely cut ties with me out of nowhere."

"I wouldn't say exactly out of nowhere..." Zoey trailed off.

"Okay. Not exactly out of nowhere. It was sort of a big snap, though. And I feel like he's lying to Beth to try and make what he and I had nothing. And it wasn't nothing. You can't be best friends with someone for that long and then just trail off and ignore them. It's like I'm being ghosted."

"You are," Zoey said. "And I'm sorry about that."

"The more I think about it, the more I realize I don't think I really loved him," I said, looking down at my hands. The dirt on them had seeped into the crevices on my fingers, and I played with it with my nails. I always had dirt on my hands, something Tobey didn't particularly like. But Tucker didn't seem to mind.

And that was nice. Not that I should compare them.

After all, Tobey had only been a friend, a relationship where something had shattered irrevocably. And Tucker was a friend. But while we might be changing everything, it wouldn't be permanent. He didn't want that, and I didn't know if I would ever be ready for something like that.

"What do you mean by that?" Erin asked, her voice soft.

"I think I wanted to love him. I think that warmth and heart and attraction I felt for him was our friendship. And it felt like we should be together. And then we weren't. I assumed that was where we needed to be. I put so much into that thinking and wishing that I don't think I knew what was real. I don't think it was love. At least not the kind that is all-encompassing and being *in* love. Because I did love him, but not in the way I should have. And not in the way he clearly didn't love me either." I frowned. "That was a lot of double negatives."

Zoey grinned. "Yes, but I followed. You loved him as your friend. Maybe something more, but you weren't *in* love with him. I get that. Believe me. I get that."

I avoided her gaze as Erin and I shared a look.

Neither of us was about to touch that with a ten-foot pole.

Especially when things were already a little secretive with my brothers.

I had to tell them. But I didn't know how.

"So, back to where we started with all of this," Zoey said. "What are you hiding?"

I looked at them and bit my lip. "Tucker and I aren't really dating," I blurted.

"You mean that you totally used him as a fake relationship so we wouldn't pity you?" Erin said deadpan.

"Maybe," I drawled out.

"Did you really know that?" I added quickly.

"Of course, we knew that," Zoey said, rolling her eyes. "But I'm surprised that Tucker went along with it. Though given that you guys have slept together, is it real now? Because that would be okay."

"Devin would be okay with it," Erin confirmed.

My heart raced, and I felt like the rug had literally been pulled out from under my feet. "Wait. Hold on. You knew this whole time? I was lying to you guys, and you let me do it?"

"We really didn't mean for that whole thing at the coffee shop to happen. We weren't going to set you up on a date. We mentioned you to that guy, but in a passing way. Then he saw you and wanted to take the next step."

"I know you guys didn't have anything to do with that. Not really. But it sort of just steamrolled into the lie. I'm so sorry."

"You don't have to be sorry," Erin said.

"Yes, I do. I lied. And that's horrible."

"But it's not a lie anymore, is it?" Zoey said.

"It is a little. I mean, we're not really dating."

"Um, you had sex face," Erin said.

"Hey. Stop talking about sex and my face at the same time. It's weird."

"Don't change the subject," Zoey said. "You and Tucker are sleeping together. Therefore, the relationship is real. Right?"

I played with my fingers, shrugging.

"It's not real-real. But it's not fake. We called it beard sex."

"I really don't want to know what kind of kinky shit you guys get into," Zoey said with a laugh.

"Oh, stop it. I called him my beard. My fake date," I added.

"Oh, that's great. When you finally tell Devin, you're going to have to mention that. He'll find that part funny," Erin said.

"Wait, so my brothers still think it's real?" I asked, worried.

Erin gave me a sad smile. "I don't know. We talked about the fact that he thought you and Tucker would be good for each other, but I didn't mention that I figured you might be lying, and he didn't either. I do not lie to the love of my life. So, you better tell him quickly. That way, I can continue not lying to the love of my life. Okay?"

I nodded. "Yes. As soon as I see them next."

Zoey raised a brow.

"Okay. Tonight. Tonight, I will tell my brothers exactly what's going on with Tucker and me. Not that I know exactly what's going on with us. But I will tell them the truth."

"And then you'll figure out what's going on between you and Tucker?" Zoey asked.

"If I knew the answer to that, maybe I wouldn't feel like I was drowning in my own thoughts and lies."

The girls helped me work a bit more, and then they left, mostly to go do their own work. But I had a feeling that I'd have to meet my brothers soon and tell them the truth. The problem was, I had no idea what I was going to say.

I felt like I needed to be punished a bit more than I had been, considering that I had been lying to their faces. Just because they hadn't believed me, didn't mean I wasn't lying.

"Knock knock," Tucker said as he walked into my greenhouse. He looked over at me and grinned. "You look gross," he said, and I flipped him off.

"Thanks, asshole."

"Hey, it's hot in here. You're all sweaty and covered in dirt. I kind of like it."

"You're weird. I did not realize you had that kink."

"I didn't either. Good to know, right?"

"So, the girls know."

Tucker nodded as he leaned against the post.

"They know about the beard thing."

"About your kink?" he asked, and I growled.

"Why did you use the word kink? Why is everyone calling it kink? It's a fake relationship."

"It's just really fun to say *kink*, and it's even more fun to watch you get all flustered about it."

"You're so mean."

"I am not. Would someone mean come here to help you with whatever you're doing in here?"

I grinned. "You're really going to get dirty?" He raised a brow, the smirk on his face doing way too many good things to my stomach and insides.

"Oh. I think I can get dirty."

"We are not having sex in this greenhouse," I said, holding up both hands.

"No. But I'm pretty sure we could use the shower later to get clean. Everywhere."

"How am I supposed to re-pot this plant when I'm thinking about your dick?" I asked, shaking my head.

"I don't know. It's a chore, isn't it? I mean, I have to go to the hospital every day and work, all the while thinking about your ass and your tits."

"You are a horrible man," I said with a laugh.

He grinned, then leaned down and kissed me, a soft one that slowly grew to more. My breasts ached, my nipples beaded against my bra, and all I wanted to do was reach around him, hold him close, and never let go.

And because of that, I took a step back and smiled.

"Okay, I am going to teach you all about replanting."

"Really? You know I've worked beside you many times. In fact, I could probably teach you a thing or two."

"Ego much?" I asked on a laugh.

"Fine, I really can't teach you anything about this. But I've helped you before. Tell me what to do, and I can get it done. I'm usually good about keeping things alive."

"That's always a good sign in our lines of work."

"Pretty much."

I frowned, looking over at him. "What's wrong?"

He shook his head, slowly stripping off his shirt. I had to keep my gaze on his face rather than down below, or I would lose my train of thought.

"Stuff at work. Can't talk about it."

"HIPAA?" I asked.

"Yeah. But let's just say it was a really bad day. So, I could use a little fun."

"I can do that."

He smiled then, and a little bit of it reached his eyes.

I didn't really want to know exactly what it was he had seen that day because it was his job to look at scans and other various things. And, sometimes, those pictures didn't tell you the best story. I got to make things grow, make people happy. Sometimes, he had to be the bearer of bad news.

So, I would make him smile. After all, it's what he helped me with day after day.

Apparently, our beard relationship could work both ways. I just had to remember not to be the selfish person Tobey thought I was.

"Okay, Tucker. You better show me how well you can use your hands," I growled out, trying to make my voice all smoky.

He threw his head back and laughed, and I fell a little bit more into whatever it was I felt for him.

It wasn't love, though. I was not going to fall in love with Tucker.

By the time we had replanted all my plants, we were both covered in dirt and sweat. And I had never laughed so hard as I had in that greenhouse.

We stumbled out, and Tucker held me close to his naked and sweaty chest.

"Have you ever had sex outside?" he asked, his voice low.

I looked around, aware that we were in the greenhouse area surrounded by trees. No one would be able to see us.

"No, but it's cold as fuck out here."

"There's no snow on the ground right here. It'll be good. I promise."

"Yeah, so said the spider to the fly."

"I'd make a joke about webbing, but that's weird."

"Oh my God," I said with a groan.

"Never again."

"I'll do my best."

"But you want to?" he asked, grinning.

"Oh, yes. That was the line. The best one ever. And totally. But we're going to have to be quiet."

"I think we can make that happen." And then his mouth was on mine, and I was sighing into him.

He already had his shirt off, and before I could blink, mine was over my head, and I stood outside in my work boots and jeans and a bra.

Apparently, having sex with Tucker meant having sex in new places.

And as his hand gripped my ass, I had a feeling new places might mean something entirely different one day.

That was if we continued doing this.

Not that I thought we would.

Because soon, it would be over, and everything would be fine. We would go back to normal. He would go on to date other people, and I would be healthier and happier and whole.

Because he had helped me get over Tobey. And that's why he was here. To help me figure out exactly who I needed to be. His words, not mine.

We weren't serious. This was all we needed.

When he pinched my ass, my eyes widened. "What was that for?"

"Be here with me, not wherever you went just then. Got me?"

I swallowed hard and nodded, and then he was kissing me again.

We slowly worked each other out of the rest of our clothes, and he made a little nest for me, so my back was on his shirt and the coat he'd brought out with him, and then he was over me, kissing me and caressing me, biting and licking.

I arched my back as he lapped at my breasts, molding them and pinching them with his fingers. He was a little rougher than I'd ever had before, yet sweet at the same time.

I ached for him, my body holding him as he hovered above me.

He slid a condom over his length, and then he was teasing my entrance, his thumb over my clit as he slowly worked his way in and out of me. I stretched for him, aching. It had been a while before him, and he was big. But it was so worth it. He hit me in all the right spots as he slowly moved. I arched for him, my fingernails digging into his back as he made love to me.

No. *Had sex.* Fucked. All the words but *love.*

Because there couldn't be that.

I wasn't going to make that mistake again.

His mouth was on mine, and then I couldn't think of anything else. He slid his hand between us, his thumb over my clit again, and I came, clamping down around him. He growled out my name as he slammed into me once more, this time my back digging in to the dirt below us. And when he came, he rolled to his back, completely missing the nest so he was on the hard dirt in a Colorado winter. And yet I rode him to completion, his hands on my breasts and my hips and then his mouth on mine again.

I whispered his name, feeling happy, a bit more whole.

Because this was okay. This didn't have to mean anything but what it was. Happiness. That's all it had to be.

As Tucker held me, as he made me laugh, I swallowed hard, worried that I was doing the one thing I shouldn't.

And I suddenly realized that I hadn't loved Tobey.

Not in truth.

But I was well on my way to falling for Tucker.

# FIFTEEN

*Tucker*

I ACTUALLY HAD THE FULL DAY OFF TODAY, SO I planned to clean my house and probably head over to Amelia's later.

I didn't know why that made me so excited, but maybe it needed to be.

I was probably making a mistake when it came to her, but I didn't think either of us was backing away anytime soon.

I didn't know what I felt for her, but I didn't think it was only a fake relationship, a beard, or even just friendship anymore.

That worried me, especially since I didn't actually want this. I didn't want a future with anyone. I wanted things to stay as they were. Because if they stayed that way, then no one would get hurt.

The doorbell rang before I could travel too far down those thoughts. I opened it, freezing as Devin strode past me, a glare on his face.

Oh, good. We were going to do this now. I probably deserved whatever happened, so I would deal.

But, Jesus Christ. I wish I had figured out what to say.

Or what Amelia wanted us to say.

Us? Since when were we an *us*?

"Hey, come right in," I said, trying to keep my voice light.

"Don't mind if I do."

"So, what do you have in mind?" I asked as I closed the door. No need to let all the heat out in this type of weather. It was cold, stormy, and even though Christmas and the rest of the holidays were coming up, it sure didn't feel like it in here.

I didn't have the time to decorate, and I didn't really want it most days anyway. I hadn't had Christmas and all that growing up. Yes, I'd had a little bit of it with Devin and them, but not enough.

But I didn't miss it. You couldn't really miss what you'd never had. What you didn't remember.

"So, you ever going to tell me why you're lying?" Devin asked, apparently going straight for the punch.

I blinked, swallowing hard. "How'd you know?"

There was only one lie between us. Because I didn't lie to him, ever.

But I had for Amelia. Why?

That was the question for the ages. And one I still didn't have the answers to.

"I knew all along. We all did."

I let out a sharp laugh and ran my hand through my hair. "That's good to know. Jesus Christ."

"Yeah. That's a really good reaction to that. Neither of you is a very good liar. And it was all a little too convenient how you were suddenly together right after Tobey did that to her."

"Do you want to hit me?"

"No. I'd never hit the guy that my sister is with. I'm not that type of brother."

"You mean a misogynistic prick who has to have a territory dispute around any woman that he claims is his?" I asked, trying to make a joke out of it.

Devin shook his head, his brows raised. "It's not a misogynistic prick thing to want to take care of your own. But I also know she can make her own decisions. I just really wish I would've been able to kick Tobey's ass because, apparently, he was not a good decision."

"No. And I'd probably hold him down for you. Or have you hold my coat."

"Good to know. So, why'd you do it? Why'd you agree to lie?"

"I don't know."

"That's a good answer." Devin laughed. "It's because she asked you to, isn't it?"

"Yeah. Pretty much. She asked, and I didn't want another reason to make her cry. So, I went along with it. But I shouldn't have lied to you. Even if you saw right through it."

"I'm glad you were there for her. We all tried to be, but I don't think we were the right people for her. I think she needed someone a little bit removed from it. Mostly because I think it's hard to trust the people that you love when someone else you loved fucks you over like that. So, don't fuck with her. You get me?"

I stuck my hands into my pockets and nodded tightly. "It's not fake now." And that was the most honest thing I could say. Because whatever we were, Amelia and me, it wasn't fake. Hadn't been in a long while. Not that I knew *what* it was now. And not that I knew if it would lead to anything else. I couldn't let it lead to anything.

But it wasn't fake.

And that scared the shit out of me.

"Okay."

"I don't want to hurt her, Devin."

"Then don't. You know, I know you're a ladies' man and all that shit."

"Not really. Not like that. I never, ever hurt anyone."

"I hope not." Devin looked at me for a bit and then gave

me a tight nod before coming closer and giving me a hug. Just a quick one, a couple of pats on the back as I tried to do the same to him. Then he took a few steps back.

"You're like a brother to me, Tucker, I hope you know that."

I swallowed, even though my throat felt thick.

"Same."

"Apparently, Amelia was never a sister to you," Devin said, laughing a bit.

"Apparently. I'm not going to hurt her." I hoped I wouldn't hurt her.

"Well, you better not. Because I haven't been able to get to Tobey. And I think it would kill me to have to kill you. Just saying."

"What about that whole giving her space so she can make her own decisions thing?"

"That was before she got hurt because I thought I was doing the right thing. And then some asshole had to be a douche to her. Who knows what else he said or thought when it came to her? I'll never forgive myself for letting her get hurt."

"Same."

"Good. Figure out what it is the two of you are. If it's casual, I don't want to hear about the details," he added quickly, and I smiled softly. "So, figure it out, and don't hurt each other. Because you're my family just as much as she is. And I don't want either of you to end up hurt in the end."

Before I could say anything else, he shook his head and walked to the door, leaving without saying another word.

I didn't think there was anything else *to* say, though. Was there?

Because I didn't want to hurt Amelia. But I had a feeling if I wasn't careful, we would end up fucking each other over in the end.

I pulled out my phone and looked down at it, wondering what I should say. I used to be better at this. Whatever *this* was.

**Me:** *Devin was just here.*

**Amelia:** *Oh my God. Are you okay?*

I leaned against the wall, shaking my head. Of course, she would be worried about me. That's who she was.

**Me:** *I'm fine.*

I thought about telling her that he knew, but I figured that was something I needed to say in person. Because I knew she wanted to tell her brothers to their faces, but I didn't really know what she would think about a text just then.

**Amelia:** *You're okay though?*

**Me:** *I'm fine. I'll see you a bit later though, right?*

**Amelia:** *That's the plan. I'm bringing dinner over, right?*

**Me:** *Yeah, bring takeout from Gurus.*

**Amelia:** *So, we'll order like seven things and then have leftovers for the next two weeks?*

I smiled.

**Me:** *Sounds perfect. See you soon.*

I put down my phone, a smile playing on my lips. This was bad. So bad.

I dated. I had fun. I didn't put too much of myself into anything. But it was hard to be that way when I was with Amelia. And I didn't know why.

It shouldn't be like that.

But, apparently, I didn't really have a choice when it came to her. And that scared me more than it should.

The doorbell rang, and I frowned, looking down at my phone. She couldn't be here already. Maybe it was Devin again. Or one of Amelia's other brothers. Considering that she had a vat of them, they'd probably all come by to threaten to kick my ass at some point. It only made sense.

I opened the door and frowned. The woman standing there had long, auburn hair tied at the nape of her neck, dark eyes with a bit of sadness to them, strong cheekbones, and a pointed chin. She was tall, had on heeled boots, a tight jacket, and her hands were closed around the strap of her purse so tightly that I could see her knuckles turning white.

And I knew this woman.

Just then, I remembered the two phone calls I'd missed, and the fact that I hadn't called her back because I'd been distracted by Amelia. And myself.

"Melinda?"

She gave me a smile that didn't reach her eyes, and I frowned again.

"I was afraid you wouldn't remember me, Tucker."

She had a sexy-as-sin voice, and a laugh that always made me laugh with her. She'd been fun, the two of us going out a few times, but we'd never had anything serious. Not that I'd ever been serious or had any plans to be, but we'd had a couple of fun nights.

I didn't even know why I still had her number in my phone since it had been a few years since I last spoke to her.

"It's cold as fuck out there, come in," I said, wondering why she was here.

She let out a shaky breath before walking past me, and unease settled in my gut.

"What's up, Melinda? Are you okay?"

"You know, I had this whole speech prepared in my head about what I would say and what I needed to do, and now it's all gone. I looked at you, and now I can't see it anymore. I can't think at all. I look at you and can only wonder how the hell I missed it. How in the hell I could have been so wrong."

I fisted my hands at my sides, trying to calm my nerves. I had no idea what she was saying, she was just rambling at this point.

"What's wrong, Melinda? I don't understand what you're talking about."

"You wouldn't. You wouldn't at all. I don't even really know. I wish you would have answered your phone. Maybe it would have been easier to say if I wasn't facing you. 'Cause every time I look at you, I see what I should have seen before. But I can see it now."

Tears filled her eyes, and I quickly moved toward her, grabbing the box of tissues from the table as I did. I handed one to her, and she gave me a watery smile before dabbing at her eyes.

"Thank you. You were always so sweet. Even though you were just fun, and it was supposed to only be a couple of nights, you were always so sweet. You weren't one of those assholes that wanted to get in my pants because I had big boobs."

I snorted then, setting the box on the coffee table. "I'd like to think I wasn't an asshole. But it's been a long time, Melinda. What, six years or so?"

"Oh, almost seven at this point." She sucked in a deep breath and then slowly let it out. I swallowed hard, a tingling sense of fear sliding down my spine.

"I need you to listen to me and let me get out the facts."

"Do you need to sit down?" I asked, my voice equally shaky at this point.

She shook her head vehemently. "No. I just need to get this out, and maybe I need to pace."

"Okay. Talk to me, Melinda."

"I have a son. His name is Evan. He's the sweetest boy."

I nodded, still a little confused. "Okay. Do you need money or something?"

"Or something. Just...just let me get this out."

"Okay."

"His name is Evan. He has acute lymphocytic leukemia."

Dread rolled in my belly. "Oh, fuck. I'm sorry, Melinda. I'm so damn sorry."

"Me, too. It's been on and off for the past year or so. We went through all the treatments, at least the initial ones. But now, we need bone marrow."

"Yeah, that's a common treatment. And acute lympho-cytic leukemia has a ninety percent five-year survival rate for children, right?"

"Yes. Ninety percent. It's a great number. It's those ten percent that's so scary."

"Because kids aren't numbers. They aren't specs on a scan. I get that." I had to get that. It was my job. I had to think analytically most days. And I knew I needed to now, as well.

"That's right, you're a radiologist or something, right? You get that."

"I do." And I hated it. I hated percentages. Hated numbers. Hated the fact that kids got cancer, and there wasn't anything I could do about it. "What can I do for you? I know a few good doctors around here. Maybe I can get you into one. Is that what you need?"

"No, we're with Dr. Bates at the Children's Medical Hospital. We're in good hands."

"I know him. He's a great physician, and a great guy."

"The best. The thing is, Evan needs bone marrow. And he needs yours."

I blinked, my blood thundering in my ears as I tried to understand what the fuck she was saying. "Excuse me?"

"I'm really not good at this."

"Why would he need mine, Melinda? How old is Evan?"

"He's six," she said, her voice breaking. She turned her phone, and I looked at a picture of a little boy with auburn hair, strong cheekbones, and my fucking eyes. My knees went weak, and I sat down on the coffee table, the glass on top rattling as I tried to catch my breath.

"What the fuck, Melinda? Are you kidding me?"

"I thought he was my boyfriend's. I was seeing someone else at the time."

"I don't get it. You're going to need to talk slower." My heart raced, and my palms went sweaty. I couldn't breathe. Couldn't think. This couldn't be happening. I was always so careful, not only with my feelings and my emotions, but also with everything else. I never wanted a child. Had never liked the idea of someone having to grow up without me because of an accident or some shit like I had with my parents. That had always been my number-one rule.

But it seemed fate was a tricky bitch and had gotten around that.

"How long have you known?"

I wasn't sure I believed her, wasn't sure I believed anything. Couldn't even get my words wrangled into complete sentences at this point. My thoughts weren't any better.

I couldn't do this. What the fuck?

My mind shut down. I was basically running on autopilot at this point. At least, I thought I was. Was I even speaking? Was I thinking?

Why did I feel like I needed to throw up?

"I lied to you. We were on a break, like Ross and Rachel, but it really wasn't. I just wanted some fun because my boyfriend and I were fighting. And you were fun."

Fun. That's what I was. Fun. Now, it looked like much more than that. But that's what I wanted, right? That's exactly what I wanted.

"I'm so sorry. But after you and I did our thing, Robbie and I got back together. We got married, and we're okay. We worked through it. And we never really thought it was cheating because he was with someone else in those couple of months, as well. But that time gave me Evan. Although because of the timing, we thought he was Robbie's. We didn't have to second-guess it. You and I were always so careful, and Robbie and I weren't. I thought he was Robbie's until we got the tests back confirming that Evan wasn't his.

We haven't been able to really think about what to do about it."

"Does Evan know?" I asked, my voice wooden.

"He does now." Her teeth worried her lower lip, her hands so tight on that purse I was afraid she might snap the leather in two. "He knows because we're still waiting on bone marrow. And the best match is someone in his familial line. And, sadly, it's not me. I can't even save my own son. I need you to help me, Tucker. I need you to help me save my child. I don't know what happens next. I don't know what you want to do. If you want to be a part of this or not. But you needed to know. And I need your help. I need to save my son. And I will do anything to ensure that. He is everything to me. Everything to me and Robbie. I didn't mean to dump all this on your shoulders and everything. But I couldn't get ahold of you, and then I remembered where you lived. I wish you would have answered your phone. Because we're running out of time. I need you to help me save my son. My baby boy. Please, help me." She cracked then, her tears falling so fast and hard that I thought she might break. I stood up and then held her close, not knowing what else to do.

She cried, and I held her, my hand rubbing up and down her back.

"Help me, Tucker. Please. Help me."

I didn't know what to say. What was there to say? Before I could do anything, the front door opened. Apparently, I hadn't closed it all the way. Amelia walked in. She met my gaze, looked down at the woman in my arms, and we all froze.

I didn't know what I was thinking, let alone what she might.

# Sixteen

*Amelia*

TUCKER STOOD IN HIS LIVING ROOM, HOLDING another woman as she cried, and yet there wasn't a single emotion on his face. I couldn't read anything in his expression honestly. He stood there with the woman in his arms, and there was...nothing.

Nothing coming from him.

And yet, something twisted inside of me.

Who was this woman? Why did this hurt so much?

This wasn't Tobey. Wasn't Beth. Even though there was a weird similarity that wasn't actually similar at all.

I'd trusted Tobey, and he had hidden something from me. I knew that now. I knew I didn't love him, but I had thought that he was what I needed.

As I stared at Tucker with this woman in his arms, I couldn't help but remember that he had been with many women before me. And that we were only in a fake relationship.

And then I felt something else. I wanted to reach out to the woman in tears. I wanted to make sure she was okay.

All of those thoughts ran through my head at the same time, turning and tumbling together, disappearing into a vast expanse of nothingness.

I couldn't help but wonder why Tucker wasn't saying anything, why he didn't seem to be feeling anything. And why his eyes looked so blank.

The woman cleared her throat and backed away.

"I'm sorry, I didn't realize you had company."

I did my best to smile and not raise my brows or react in any kind of jealous way. I shouldn't be jealous. Tucker wasn't mine. "I guess I could say the same. I'm sorry."

"No, I am. I'm Melinda. I just needed to talk to Tucker for a bit." She reached out her hand. I looked at it for a moment before taking it and giving it a shake.

"Amelia."

"Nice to meet you." She smiled, but there was such deep sadness in her eyes that I wanted to reach out and hug her, as well.

What had been going on here?

She looked at Tucker. "You have my number. Please, call me. Soon."

She gave me a watery smile and then walked out, leaving Tucker and me alone.

Tucker looked at me for a minute, and neither of us said anything.

It wasn't like he was cheating. You couldn't cheat on something we didn't have.

Right?

"It's not what you think," he said, and I blinked.

That wasn't at all what I'd expected him to say.

"It's okay," I said quickly. "We made no promises."

That hadn't been the right thing to say, and I knew it. Not with the way his eyes filled with anger. Then his expression went back to that one of darkness that didn't really say anything at all.

"You're right," he said, letting out an angry laugh.

"Tucker."

"No, you're right. We didn't make any promises. Other than the fact that I said I didn't cheat. Ever. But I'm not Tobey. I'm not going to keep secrets from you. So, don't be like that, okay?"

There was such anger in his tone, a biting bark, that I took a step back, not even realizing that I had done it until his eyes narrowed.

I knew he didn't cheat. He was a good man.

But the whole thing threw me off balance. And, yes, maybe I had put some of my own feelings about Tobey in the middle of it all, but that didn't mean I was in the wrong here. There was no wrong here. Right?

"What's wrong, Tucker? Who is Melinda, and why was she here?"

"She's here because her son is sick."

I frowned, shaking my head. "Sick?"

His words didn't really make sense to me, and I felt like I was three steps behind, trying to catch up even though there wasn't really anything to catch up to.

"Sick as in cancer. Leukemia. The kid needs a bone marrow transplant."

"And you can help with that? Do you know someone at the hospital?"

He gave a hollow laugh. "I love that your mind went to the same place as mine. No, they have a doctor. What they need is bone marrow. From the kid's biological dad."

He looked at me then, his face completely pale and emotionless. I tried to comprehend his words.

"You're saying...you're saying you had a baby with her?" I asked, my voice shaky. "And you had no idea?"

"Of course, I didn't know. If I had known, I'd have done something about it a long time ago. You know that."

"Of course, I do. Tucker, you told me what you went through. About the different foster homes."

"Yeah, Devin became my family. You all did. I would never put a kid through what I went through. Not knowing his past or feeling like he was abandoned or some shit. And now he's sick. And, apparently, I'm supposed to do something."

"Tucker," I whispered, and then I moved forward.

He didn't open his arms, didn't reach out to me, so I didn't do anything either. I just stood in front of him, feeling as helpless as he looked.

Tucker. A dad.

Dear God.

There was a kid out there that looked like him, that needed him, and that woman that had been in his arms and crying, had been crying for her son. Grieving so much.

And I had no idea what to say. What was there to say about this?

"So she came to you today?"

"Yeah. She called a couple of times before, but I was distracted at the time. I kept telling myself I'd call back, but then I forgot."

The way he said it, I knew exactly what he'd been distracted by. Me.

He hadn't answered her calls, hadn't seen what she wanted because he'd been dealing with my issues.

And that little kid had been sick the entire time, neither of us paying attention to anyone but ourselves.

Bile filled my throat, but I swallowed it, knowing I couldn't carry the world on my shoulders even though I really wanted to make things better. But I didn't know how.

"Did she know before this?"

"No. She thought the kid was her boyfriend's. Apparently, she was dating both of us. Who knew? Apparently, I didn't cheat, but she did. But that's not the important thing. She and her boyfriend, well, her husband now, raised that little boy. And he's sick. Apparently, they need to see if I'm a match. If all this stuff is actually real. For all I know, I'm not the dad, and she was with someone else or some shit."

"What are you going to do?"

"I don't fucking know."

I closed the distance between us, wrapping my arms around his waist, and he stood still for a moment before hugging me back.

I let out a relieved breath and rubbed his back, wanting to make things okay but not knowing how to do so.

I didn't think there was a way to be okay after this.

"I don't know if he's really my kid. Even though he looks like me. And I don't know what that means. I don't know if we're going to be a match or if I can help him. Or what's going to happen after all of this. I just don't fucking know. I was always so careful, Amelia."

"I know. You are. You're a good man, Tucker. You'll figure this out."

"You say that, but I feel like I'm never going to figure this fucking shit out. Jesus Christ, there's a kid out there that could be mine. And I didn't know."

"I'm sorry, Tucker. You'll figure it out. We'll figure it

out." I tried to calm my thoughts, but they were going in so many different directions, I said the only thing I could. "Let's talk to Devin. He's your best friend. He'll know what to do. He always knows what to do."

I pulled back so I could look at him, and he gave me a wooden smile. "Yeah, he always seems to know everything. He knew about us."

I froze.

"What?"

"He knew it was a lie the whole time. They all did. Apparently, they wanted to see what we would do. I knew I shouldn't have lied to him. I guess this is my karma. Lies just build up on each other and then you end up in a world where you have no idea what the fuck's going on."

"So he knew."

They all did. But I couldn't deal with that right then. I would deal with it later, apologize, and do what I needed to do. But Tucker needed me now. Right?

I might not know what we were to each other, but I could try and figure out what we needed to be together in this moment. He couldn't do this alone. We were his family, right? I would be there for him. I would try to help him.

"Okay, let me help. We'll figure out what it means that they all knew or whatever. But right now, let's go talk to Devin."

"I will." He looked at me then, his voice devoid of

emotion, so calm that it chilled. "Guess it means this is over, right?" he asked, his words not his own.

Something twisted inside my heart, and I frowned at him. "What do you mean?"

"Everyone knows. There's no need to continue the fake relationship thing. You have better things to do. Work and all that. And I, apparently, have things I need to work through. So, it's over. You get your space, and I'll figure out what I need to do."

Ice slid through me as my fingers tingled. My heart beat quickly. "Oh. Yeah."

What we had was fake. Just fun shit that had become something more. Because that's what we both needed. But there were rules. Nothing real.

If it had been real, I would have been okay staying here to try and make things better for him. I would have been able to help.

But that's not how things worked. That's not how things ever worked.

Tucker needed space. Needed to do this on his own and figure out exactly what to do about the possibility of having a son and everything that came with it. He didn't need me and my problems on top of that.

"Call Devin. I'm going to go. Leave you alone."

Why wasn't I crying? I felt like I should be crying, my eyes stung, and my heart hurt, but I didn't let even one tear fall. I simply looked at him. I wanted things to be better, but I really wasn't good at this.

I'd never been good at this.

"Yeah, you should go. I'll talk to you later."

"I'm sure."

And then I walked away, leaving him behind.

Just as we'd been when we started this arrangement, we'd end up friends. No matter what.

But it wasn't the same. And I didn't think we would end up where we should.

But I couldn't worry about my heart, about the fact that it was breaking again. Or that I felt as if I were drowning.

Because I wasn't the center of the story here.

That little boy and whatever Tucker was dealing with was.

Tucker didn't need me. He had Devin, and he had himself.

I would only be in the way.

"Tucker doesn't need me," I said aloud to myself. He didn't want me.

But I would be fine.

I just hoped that I wouldn't break again. And if Tucker truly needed to reach out, he knew that I'd be there for him.

But I didn't know if he would take that step.

# SEVENTEEN

*Tucker*

THE CHRISTMAS MUSIC PLAYING IN THE HALLS OF the hospital made my teeth hurt and reminded me I hadn't really slept in the days since Melinda had first come by.

I knew they did it because it was Christmas Eve and the holidays were here, and some people needed joy, but all I could do was wonder why the hell they thought this was okay.

Children were crying in some of the rooms, parents trying to be stoic when they didn't have answers.

Overworked doctors and nurses and lab techs and radiologists milled about. There was just so much pain and sadness in this hospital, the same one I worked in, that playing Christmas music seemed almost obtuse.

But then I remembered the smiling little girl as one of my coworkers, dressed as Santa, visited each child to give them a gift.

Hanukkah had been over for a couple of days, but there had been an electric menorah for the children, as well. There were many holidays celebrated within these halls because sometimes you had to cling to what was good, what was right, and what made children smile when it felt like there was no hope in the darkness.

It was just odd to think that, sometimes, there *was* no hope in that darkness. Perhaps I would need to figure out my own hope.

"Are you okay?" Robbie asked as he took a seat next to me in the hall.

I looked at the man who had raised Evan, who had married Melinda, and who seemed like a good guy. I tried to figure out what he must be thinking right then.

The little boy that he had raised, who he'd held the day he was born, was sick—and he couldn't help him.

I didn't know what I would do in that situation, I felt like I was merely going through the motions now, like a robot with nothing inside as I made decisions and figured out what to do.

"I should ask how you're doing," I said, looking over at the man. He had a full beard, one that he hadn't taken care of in a while it seemed, but there wasn't much time for that. Not when Evan was in and out of hospitals, and today, he'd actually been admitted and wouldn't be released again this year.

Instead, Evan and his family would be spending Christmas and into the New Year in the hospital. But, hopefully, the little boy would be able to walk out on his own power one day soon.

Not that I had met him yet.

No, we were waiting on that.

I hadn't talked to Amelia these last four days. Hadn't called Devin. Hadn't talked to anyone.

I was such a fucking idiot.

But I didn't know what to say to them. And maybe that's why Amelia had wanted to make up that big lie because she hadn't known what to do.

She'd made the wrong choice, and I'd helped her do it, yet I wasn't doing any better now.

Why was it so easy to help others, but when it came to yourself, you couldn't do a damn thing and just wanted to hide?

But that was me. It's what I had done my entire life. After all, if I didn't lean on anyone, if I didn't rely on them, they couldn't let me down.

My parents had died, and even though it wasn't their fault, some part of me had blamed them when I was a kid.

Because they were gone, and I'd needed them.

There hadn't been a damn thing I could do about it.

And then nobody wanted a kid with asthma. Nobody wanted a kid with night terrors and all that shit.

So, I'd stayed with the state until they kicked me out on my eighteenth birthday.

I had Devin's family now—well, at least I had been when we'd been kids.

But I wasn't using them.

I was ignoring Devin's calls. Something I hated, but as I didn't know what to say, that's what ended up being best. Maybe.

He had told me that he would kick my ass if I hurt Amelia, and I remembered the look on her face when I told her to get out. Even while not using those exact words, I figured I'd hurt her.

She would be better off without me, though.

Better off without all my new complications for sure. And as a man who didn't like complications, who actively avoided them, this put me way out of my comfort zone.

I didn't know what to do next.

All I did know was that I didn't want to put any of the responsibility on Amelia's shoulders.

And I didn't know how I was going to face her brothers.

My best fucking friends.

But Devin wasn't here, mostly because no one knew where *I* was.

If he had known, he'd probably be here.

But I was good at hiding, proficient at doing things on my own.

"You okay? No, that's really not a good question, is it? You seem so lost."

I cleared my head of my thoughts and looked over at Robbie.

"It seems like everything is happening all at once and yet not fast enough," I said, leaning back in my chair.

Robbie let out a humorous laugh. "Tell me about it. We've been dealing with this for a year or so now. I don't even know how long it's been any more, truth be told. Melinda could give you the dates. She knows every one to come, too. Every piece of data, everything she has to know about the doctors. That's what she's good at, you know? The organizing and the math and anything that she can put her hands on."

"I didn't know that," I said, holding back a wince.

"No, I don't suppose you did. You two really weren't a couple or anything."

There was no censure in the man's tone, nothing that belayed the fact that maybe Melinda and I had cheated, even though, technically, they hadn't been together at the time.

Everything was so fucking complicated, but there was no more running from it. No more hiding.

"No. I didn't really get to know her like I should have."

I didn't really get to know any of the women I'd been with. Except for Amelia. I knew her.

But that didn't matter. Because of the big mistake. No matter how many times I told myself that it had to be fake, I thought maybe it wasn't. And I'd told Devin I wouldn't hurt her, but it didn't matter in the end.

Because I had.

And there was no fixing that.

"Well, I'm kind of glad you didn't get to know her. Because if you had, she wouldn't have come back to me."

"I'm glad you have her. You have each other."

"Me, too. Before Evan came along, she was the best thing in my life. Our fight that made us break up was so stupid. About school, of all things." I frowned, looking over at him. "I wanted to go back to school, something I didn't end up doing in the end because I got a promotion at work and everything worked out. But she didn't want to put her career on hold and pay for me to go or some shit like that. It was just so stupid because I would have figured it out on my own. But she thought that we needed to do it together, even though it didn't all fall on her. It didn't really matter in the end, though, because she came back, and we had each other. And then Evan."

"Yeah, you had Evan."

"You're going to meet him soon, that much I can promise you."

"And you're okay with that?"

Robbie shrugged, not looking at me.

"I would say I don't really have a choice, but I do. And

so does Melinda. And so does Evan. But Evan knows that I'm not his biological dad. That's the data, something we couldn't hide from him because, even though he's a little boy, he wanted to know why my bone marrow didn't match, and why Melinda's wasn't good. I don't know if we made the right decision in telling him, but we can't go back now. So, he knows that I'm not his dad."

"And he knows that I am," I said, letting those words settle. The test results had come back. I was Evan's biological father. I'd be meeting him today.

Melinda had wanted me to, said that I needed to see the little boy that I would hopefully be helping.

I didn't know what to think. Didn't know what would happen next. But if Melinda needed me to help her kid, I'd figure it out.

Because I wasn't going to let my problems, my insecurities, make a little boy hurt any more than he already was.

That was the only thing I could promise.

I didn't have much left, after all.

"Evan's a great kid, the light of my life. Melinda and I thought about having another child about a year ago. We love him so much, we wanted Evan to have a little brother or sister. And then all of this happened, and things got complicated. But he's a good boy. And I think you'll like him. He's funny, sweet, a little tired right now, but he still has so much energy in those eyes of his that you know he'd rather be running around, chasing me, or playing a game outside."

"I really hope he gets to do all of that soon," I said, my throat tight. "I really hope so."

"Well, we'll figure it out."

"I'm going to donate, Robbie. No matter what happens after, that part you don't need to worry about."

Robbie's shoulders sagged, and he nodded. "Melinda said you would. She was worried at first, but she said she remembered how you sometimes talked about your patients. At least in the general sense. She said you're caring. And the fact that you're here at all says that. We figured you'd try. Or figure it out. Because Evan can't go anywhere. Especially now."

Tears slid down the man's face, but I didn't reach out to comfort him. If he had been one of my friends, I would have, tears didn't scare me. Robbie just needed a moment to himself, so I turned away, waiting for Melinda to come back. She was in Evan's room, getting him ready to meet me, though I didn't know if Christmas Eve was the best time for that.

I'd brought Evan a present. A book I'd liked when I was a kid, one I hadn't been able to keep while in the foster homes. But I'd liked it.

I knew I wanted the boy to have it. Maybe. Maybe he wouldn't like it at all.

I had been a little bit younger than Evan when I lost everything. Now, I could only hope that this little boy had a chance.

I didn't know exactly what would happen next.

"Tucker? Are you ready?"

I stood up, my knees shaking, my palms damp. I tucked the wrapped book against my side and nodded. "As long as he is."

Melinda gave me a sad smile, but there was real hope in her eyes.

Hopefully, it wasn't for naught.

"He is. Let's go, he's excited to meet you."

"Really? And he knows who I am?"

"In a sense. He's a little too young to understand everything, but he knows that you were my friend before. And that you guys have the same blood type, and some other very similar things. And that you are his daddy, too, just not in the same way that Robbie's his daddy."

My heart sped up, and I swallowed hard, not a single word coming to mind.

Other than *daddy*.

Jesus.

"You don't have to be anything you don't want to be after this. You can leave and never come back after you donate. You don't even have to walk in there if you don't want to. You don't have to be anything to us or Evan other than a donation. *But* if you go in there right now, you need to be strong. He needs that. And then we'll figure out what happens later. You can be his friend. You can be anything. We'll figure out the legalities and the labels and everything after my son is healthy. Because that is all that matters to me."

I nodded quickly and watched as she sighed in relief as Robbie hugged his wife close, kissing the top of her head. "We'll deal with all the mundane things later. But first, let's try to have a Merry Christmas Eve. Okay, darling?"

She looked up at him then, and I saw the love that had never been there for me. I hadn't needed that from her, and she hadn't needed it from me.

But I saw that emotion now.

Something that I had seen in Amelia, too. Maybe. Or maybe I was thinking too hard because I didn't want to think about what was on the other side of that door.

But then I didn't have time to think it all because Melinda was opening the door, and my feet were moving, and there were no more words.

Evan sat in his bed, the back raised so he was sitting upright.

He had an IV in his arm, and wires everywhere. I knew every single name of those machines, I knew the drug that was going through his system, I knew why he was being hydrated, I knew exactly why he had dark circles under his eyes.

I knew all the medical terms and all the things that could go wrong, but it didn't matter. Because he wasn't his disease. He wasn't just a statistic.

This was Evan.

My son.

And holy hell, that was a weird thought.

"Hey," I said, my voice hoarse. I cleared my throat. "Hey, Evan. I'm Tucker."

Evan grinned, his eyes bright if a little tired. "Hi. Mommy said you'd be here. I'm Evan."

"It's nice to meet you."

Evan smiled as his mom and dad went to the other side of the bed, Melinda reaching out to hold his hand. His tiny little hand.

Jesus Christ, this little boy had to be okay.

I didn't know what I would do if I lost him just when I met him. Let alone what Melinda and Robbie would do or feel.

I looked into Evan's eyes, the same eyes as mine, and I immediately loved this kid.

Just like that. It was love at first sight. I had no idea what I would be in his life, what labels we would use for each other or any shit like that. But it didn't matter.

This kid in front of me? This was the connection that I had been waiting for in my life.

One that I had told myself I didn't need or want. The thing that I had been actively leaving and avoiding my entire life.

And he was right here in front of me. And I knew I could never walk away.

"I have a book for you," I said, looking down at the

wrapped package. "It looks like a book even wrapped, so it's not really a surprise. But I'd love to talk to you about it."

"Books? I love books."

I took a few steps and sat down next to him. I looked into those sad little eyes that still had happiness in them despite everything going on around him.

And I knew that, somehow, we'd be okay.

Because I refused to let it be anything else.

I met Melinda's and Robbie's gazes then nodded tightly before turning my attention back to Evan.

He was the important thing.

Just him.

Not anything else going through my mind.

Him.

And I was honestly okay with that.

I stayed at the hospital for a full hour before Evan fell asleep, then I left Melinda and Robbie with their son.

Since they were in the children's ward, and it was a holiday, both of them could stay overnight rather than only one of them.

I was glad that they had each other, and I was even happier that I had a moment to breathe, to try and make sense of my emotions.

I made it home, Christmas Eve, right around dinnertime, and I was alone. It's what I was good at.

No, that wasn't right. I'd always had Devin and his

family. I wasn't alone. But right then, I felt alone, mired in a turmoil of my own making.

Because I had pushed Amelia away. Like I'd said I wouldn't.

It was fucking Christmas Eve.

I'd bought her a goddamn present the week before. A little thing to put a smile on her face, something that she could hang in her bedroom so it would catch the light and make her happy before she went outside and did what she did. Because she could make life with her hands, and she brought joy to people.

And I had hurt her.

Because I'd been scared and wanted to be alone.

I had done the exact thing Tobey had done to her. I had kicked her out because I was fucking scared and a jerk and an idiot.

Jesus Christ. It was Christmas Eve, and I had no idea what she was doing, what she was feeling because I couldn't even make sense of my own thoughts.

Somehow...somehow I had fallen in love with Amelia Carr, and I hadn't even realized it.

It was only supposed to be a fake relationship. A bit of fun until she was okay and ready to move on.

But I didn't want her to move on. I wanted her with me.

And I had ruined it all.

Then I thought about Evan and the fact that good days in our future weren't guaranteed.

I had no idea how things would turn out. I didn't know what would happen next in my life, but I knew I couldn't do it alone.

I had to do it with my friends.

With the people who'd always been beside me.

And the woman that I had somehow fallen in love with, even though I'd told myself I shouldn't. Jesus Christ, just because I thought I *had* to do everything on my own, didn't mean that was the case.

I hadn't wanted to get married or have kids because I was afraid of losing them. And yet, here I was, with someone in my life who could *die*, and I'd only met them recently. There was no walking away from this. No running from the life I could have had if I hadn't been a fucking idiot. All of my reasons for being who I was, for the decisions I made, fell out from under me. I knew I had fucked up.

I needed to find Amelia. Had to fix this.

As the snow started to fall, and the lights twinkled on the houses all around mine, I knew it was now or never.

Because there were no more tomorrows for some, and I wanted my coming days to be spent with her.

I had to see her, even if she sent me away like I deserved.

# EIGHTEEN

*Amelia*

THE SONG ON THE RADIO WAS TELLING ME TO have a merry little Christmas, and all I could do was try and keep the tears at bay.

I was such a mess. Seriously. A mess.

I wasn't the same person I had been even a month before, not by a long shot. But I was still a mess. Because I was alone.

Like always. But this time, it felt even worse.

My phone chirped next to me, and I look down at it, surprised to see Tobey's name.

I swallowed hard.

**Tobey**: *Merry Christmas. I hope you have a good holiday.*

Was it odd that I didn't feel anything right then? Shouldn't I? I didn't, though. Tobey wasn't the man I thought he was. And maybe that was on me since I'd only seen what I wanted to. But in the end, it didn't matter. I couldn't be the person he needed me to be, and he surely wasn't the man I needed.

**Me**: *Merry Christmas.*

I didn't say anything else. There wasn't much more to say. He didn't reply, and that was fine. Tobey was in my past. Not part of my future. And that was something I'd had to learn the hard way. But I wasn't alone. Not truly.

I was surrounded by family, this Christmas Eve filled with dog barks and laughter and wine.

My family was everything. They had always been there for me, and I'd almost forgotten that and tried to push them away.

Sure, like me, they were a little pushy and wanted to make sure they were always there, and sometimes it was a little too much.

But because I had pushed them like I had, I'd almost lost myself. And I'd allowed myself to make bad decisions.

I'd allowed myself to lie and to fall in love with someone I shouldn't.

Dear God, how flaky was I?

I'd thought I loved Tobey, so I had told him in the most over-the-top fashion, thinking that's what he would want, but I had been wrong. Horribly wrong.

And, somehow, I hadn't seen beneath the surface. Hadn't truly seen the man he was, and I didn't like that man.

I didn't like who I saw when I didn't have my rose-colored glasses on.

So, I had lost my best friend.

And now Tucker. Dear God, Tucker.

He had been there for me when I needed him, had always been there for me. And, somehow, I had messed that up, too.

I loved him.

How was that even possible?

We had known each other for years, but I'd thought of him as only a friend. Nothing more. But I had been wrong.

I'd always been attracted to him, but it had turned into something more as we danced around each other and went on our strange journey toward one another.

And then when it seemed he needed me the most, he had pushed me away.

And I hadn't known how to go back to him afterwards to try and help.

Because what if I was wrong? What if I made the same mistakes as I had with Tobey and messed it all up even more?

I didn't think he loved me. Because that hadn't been in the cards. It had been a rule. And because of that, I would simply let him lean on his other friends, let him depend on

Devin because I would not be the person who ruined another friendship because of my feelings.

Even if I wasn't sure what I felt anymore.

"Okay, enough of that," Thea said as she sat down next to me, handing me a glass of wine. I looked at my sister-in-law and just grinned. "You look cheery."

"I can't help it. I love this family. And I love that you're all coming down to the Springs tomorrow to celebrate Christmas with the Montgomerys."

"Well, as long as it's not all of you."

"Hey, it's only the immediate family. And all their spouses. My cousins aren't going to be down there. Don't worry, you will not be completely inundated."

"Only a little bit," Dimitri said, laughing.

"See? Everything's fine. Now, have a sip of your wine, and then come and open your present."

"I still find it weird that you guys open a single present on Christmas Eve," Erin said, shaking her head. "We always used to open all of our presents on Christmas Eve and save one for Christmas morning."

"Well that's just strange," Caleb said, leaning against the doorway. "Like, really strange. Are you sure you're not like some pod person?"

"You're lucky my sister is with her husband's family, or she would kick your ass for that comment," Erin said as she leaned into Devin's side.

Devin kissed the top of her head before looking at me, giving me a worried glance.

I smiled brightly, hoping it reached my eyes. Because I was fine. No one needed to worry about me anymore. We all needed to worry about Tucker. The elephant in the room. Or rather, the elephant *not* in the room since he wasn't here. He had been invited. Devin had sent him a text a few days ago and had even sent him another recently. But he hadn't come. Hadn't contacted anyone either.

Nobody knew if he had gotten the test results back or if he was donating bone marrow or even how the little boy was doing.

"Before we go more into the weirdness of our families, I want to say something," Devin said, and Caleb and Dimitri looked at each other.

"Okay," I said quickly. "What?"

"Tucker's not here."

"I know. And I'm sorry."

"Oh, shut up," Caleb snapped. "It's not your fault."

"It's a little my fault," I said quickly.

"No. It's not your fault. He's going through something, and when he goes through shit, he pushes people away. He's always been like that. Even before you two got together." Devin narrowed his eyes. "And don't apologize for the lying or whatever. I know you two ended up being together for real."

"I don't know if that's the case," I said, my voice shaking

a bit. Then I swallowed hard and ignored it. I could be strong for this. "And that doesn't matter."

"It *does* matter," Zoey said, coming to stand behind Caleb. I noticed that the two pointedly didn't look at each other. Something was going on there, and I really didn't understand it. But I had my own problems to deal with, and I wasn't going to get in the middle of theirs. Not unless they needed me to or asked.

Great, I was becoming the exact type of person I tried to push away. Maybe I shouldn't have pushed them away to begin with.

"As I was saying," Devin continued, "Tucker isn't here. I'm giving him today. But tomorrow? I'm going over to his house to make sure he's okay."

"We're going, too," Caleb and Dimitri said at the same time, then looked at each other before shrugging.

"If you want me to go, I'll go. I just don't know if he wants to see me," I said, looking down at my hands.

Thea reached out and gripped my hand before taking the wine glass away and putting it down on the table.

"Okay, this is the plan. All of us as a group go over and bombard him tomorrow, and then we bring him down to the Montgomerys."

Everyone stopped talking and looked over at Thea, who shrugged.

"What? We've all gone through shit, and sometimes, it takes a big group of loud friends on a holiday for you to smile a bit. I'm sorry that he's going through all of this, though since a few of us have gone through our own versions of hell, I can tell you that sometimes you just need to be forced into being loved. It's the only way to fix it."

Dimitri leaned down and kissed his wife on the lips before whispering something into her ear that I couldn't hear.

"I don't know what to do," I said, sighing.

"He needs us," Devin said. "It might be a good idea because I don't really know what else to do. I hate that he's hurting and pushing us away."

"I did the same thing to you guys, and I'm sorry."

"Tobey was a dick," Zoey said, and Caleb looked down at her and smiled. They shared a look and then quickly looked away.

Interesting. Again, I wasn't going to get in the middle of it.

"Yes, he was a dick. But that's not important now. What's important is Tucker. I need to make sure he's all right."

"Good."

"And if I have to kick his ass for hurting you, I will do that after we make sure he's okay," Caleb said casually, and my other two brothers nodded sagely.

"You don't get to do that," I said quickly.

"Oh, we do. It's our prerogative."

Thea sighed. "It really is," she said, and Erin and Zoey nodded, as well.

"We're just friends. That's it."

"We're not going to go into the details of why you two aren't only friends because I don't want to have to gouge my eyes out," Caleb began. "But you're not. And you're hurting right now. I don't know if it's because Tobey's not here or if it's Tucker."

"Way to make me sound like I'm full of drama," I said, a little annoyed.

"That's not what I meant," Caleb grumbled, and Zoey glared at him.

"We're all used to them being here. Tobey's not here because he's a dick, and I'll continue saying that."

"I can't believe I was so wrong about him."

"We all were," Devin said. "But he's gone now. And fine. Fuck him. But the important thing is that you're here with us. And we're going to make sure Tucker is, too. You two can figure out what the fuck's going on between you later. But the main thing is that we need to make sure he's okay. Because he's family. Part of this weird, strange little family that we made."

I sighed, nodded, and then the doorbell rang.

We all looked at each other, and tension gripped my belly.

"I have a feeling you'd better get that," Dimitri said,

looking directly at me. "It might be nothing, but there are Christmas miracles and all of that."

I bit my lip and stood up, leaving the rest of them in the living room, even though I knew they would likely follow me soon. I walked to the foyer and looked through the peephole, to make sure it wasn't an ax murderer or something.

Then I sighed and opened the door. And just looked at him, wondering what the hell I was going to do.

I loved him. So damn much.

I never meant to.

I hadn't meant to fall at all.

"Tucker," I whispered.

He looked at me then, a gift in his hand, his hair messy as if he'd run his hands through it over and over.

"You're here," he whispered and took a step forward before freezing.

That's when I noticed that all three of my brothers were right behind me, glowering over my head.

"I've got this," I said, trying to put a little sternness into my tone.

"We'll see," Caleb growled.

"Yeah," Dimitri added.

"You okay?" Devin asked, looking directly at Tucker.

"I'll be okay. We'll talk later?" Tucker asked, looking over my head.

I angled myself so I could look at my brother, who

simply nodded and then tugged the others out of the way before pushing me through the front door.

I stumbled over my feet and landed right in Tucker's arms. Before I could yell at Devin, he slammed the door, the lock snicking closed.

"What the hell?" I asked, completely surprised.

Tucker snorted and shook his head.

"I swear to God, the Carr siblings are not subtle at all."

"I guess not."

I quickly scrambled away, wrapping my arms around my body. It was snowing outside, and I wasn't wearing a coat.

Not the smartest thing, but it wasn't like I had been given a choice.

Tucker cursed under his breath and set the gift down on the step before taking off his jacket and sliding it over my shoulders. He wore a turtleneck sweater, so he was at least a little warm, but I knew neither of us could stand out here for long.

"Hey," I said, my voice soft.

"Hey. I should have been here earlier. I had an appointment, and then I had my head up my ass. Hell, I've had my head up my ass for far too long."

"An appointment?" I asked, not bothering to talk about the last part of what he'd said. I wasn't really sure what I could say to that anyway.

"Yeah, I needed to get some test results back and meet Evan."

My eyes widened, my mouth going dry. "Yeah?"

Tucker slid his hands into his pockets, and I inhaled the scent of him on his jacket, my body heating even as longing slid through me.

"Yeah. He's a great kid. I read to him a bit, talked with his folks. Set another appointment to get my bone marrow donated and all that. He's mine. I don't know what the fuck's going to happen next, but he's mine. I looked at him once and fell in love with the kid." Tears filled my eyes, just like his, and I blinked them away.

"Really?"

Tucker nodded tightly. "Yeah. He's mine. Well, he's Robbie's and Melinda's, but I think a little part of him is mine, too. Like I said, I don't know what's going to happen next, but I'll figure it out. You know? As long as Evan's okay. That's the important part."

"Of course. So, you're a match? You're going to be able to donate?"

"Yeah. There was no question about that. That was the one thing that I knew I could do. Give what I could of myself to help him. Even if he wasn't mine, or I didn't know what to do about him being mine. But, yeah, Merry fucking Christmas, right?"

Tears slid down my cheeks, and he leaned forward, wiping them away with his thumb.

"Don't cry, baby. It's going to be okay. We're going to fight this."

"He's got you in his corner. And all of us Carrs. Dear God, that kid's going to have so much family now," I said, my voice shaky.

Tucker smiled, and it reached his eyes. "Yeah. So much family. I really shouldn't have pushed you guys away. All the Carrs are my family. The people in my life who have always been there. I should have let you guys be a part of this."

I nodded, trying to think of words to say because it was the truth. Even though it hurt at the same time. "Yeah. We're always here for you."

He cupped my face, and I really didn't want him to tell me it was over again. I didn't want him to tell me that we would always be friends and that, no matter what, we would be in each other's lives. Because I didn't know if I wanted only that. I had lied to myself thinking that everything would be okay once we walked away.

It couldn't be.

But I couldn't say those words.

"They're my family. But you? You're something different. I don't know how it happened, but somehow, you weren't just my best friend's little sister anymore. You were something more. You're fun and you're feisty and you're amazing. You're brilliant and beautiful, and I love you being in my life. I love spending time with you. I love cooking with you and watching stupid movies with you. I love trying to figure out what we're going to do for the day during the off hours we actually have. I want to be able to talk to you about Evan and about your brothers and everything else. I want to figure out who we are and where we go from here. I don't want to walk away again. I don't want to be fucking Tobey."

I was fully crying then, hope blooming inside me so fiercely that it scared me. "I want all of that, too. But that's not what we promised. I don't want to mess this up."

"Then we don't. We never lie again. We always tell each other what we're feeling and what we're doing. We make sure the others around us know who we are and what we are to each other. Even as we figure that out. Because what I'm facing, baby? I don't want to do it without you. I don't know what it means, and we don't need to put labels on it now. But I don't want to do it alone. Because, somehow, I fell in love with you, even though I told myself I shouldn't. Even though I knew it was the reckless choice. But I love you so fucking much."

I was full-on crying then, unable to hold back my tears. He smiled at me and then leaned down to pick up the gift.

"I figured I should give you your present now, too."

I blinked, wiping away my tears as I looked at the box.

"I don't have yours. I couldn't bring it out of the closet." My throat hurt, and I sniffed, knowing I was a mess.

I was always a mess. But, apparently, he had fallen in love with me regardless.

"It's fucking cold out here, so I'll show it to you later, but it's a light catcher. One that you can put in your bedroom and watch the rainbows twinkle off your walls when you wake up in the morning. You'll bring a little bit of the outside in."

I held the box close and smiled at him, emotions running through me so fast and quick that it was hard to keep up.

"I got you a dream catcher so, apparently, we were on the same page."

"Really?" he asked, his eyes dark.

"Yeah. So you never have to deal with your nightmares again. I know it's silly, but I saw it and thought of you."

"It's perfect, Amelia. It's going to be perfect."

"I'm not perfect, I'm far from it."

"Same here. And that's why we're going to work. It's why we're going to make this work." He paused. "If you want. Because you haven't really said anything."

"I'm not very good at that," I said honestly. "The last time I told someone I loved them, it wasn't actually what I felt."

He nodded, his eyes dimming a little. I was messing this up. I really needed to be better.

"I thought I knew what love was. I thought I knew what I needed to be with someone else. But then when I got to know you better, as I started to feel something for you, I knew that what I felt for that other person paled in comparison to what I feel for you. You are my person. You are the one who makes me smile and want more. You're the one who makes me laugh and fans this heat inside of me that's not just attraction. It's more. It makes me want to figure out who I am, and I know I won't be alone if I do that."

"I'm never going to leave like that again. I'll never push you away. I will do better. That much I can promise you."

"I love you, Tucker. I know we shouldn't have fallen this fast. I know it doesn't make any sense. But I love you. And I can't wait to figure out exactly what happens next. And see how we'll fight whatever comes. I'll always be by your side. No matter what."

That was a promise I could make. A promise that I knew I would keep no matter what.

He smiled and leaned over me, and my family started screaming and hooting and hollering from behind me in the house.

I rolled my eyes, used my finger to flip them off over my shoulder, and then laughed as Tucker's lips pressed against mine.

He kissed me with abandon, even though the others were watching. I ignored them.

Because this was my future, this was my decision.

I had made mistakes before, and I knew I would likely make some again, but I wouldn't have to deal with them alone.

I would walk my path, and I would figure out our path.

There would always be more to come—this was just the beginning.

I had been reckless more than once in my life, but never in my wildest dreams did I think it would lead me here.

To the one person I knew I could lean on, the one I knew could be my forever.

Even if I hadn't expected it.

# Epilogue

*Tucker*

"Take it, take it all," I growled, slowly working in and out of her.

She moaned, wiggling as I paused, making sure she was ready for me.

"Now, Tucker. Stop teasing." She looked up at me with wide eyes, her mouth parted. So, I *moved*.

This was our first time in this particular position, and though we'd played with toys and fingers before, my cock in her ass was on a whole different level. I watched her face as I moved, looking for any indication that this wasn't what she wanted or needed.

But she just begged for more. And because I loved her,

because I needed her, because she was everything to me, I gave it to her.

I leaned down, working my hips as I sucked on her breasts before going up to her mouth, needing her taste.

She clung to me, her body arching as I moved, and when I slid my fingers between us and over her clit, her fingernails dug into my back.

"Tucker," she breathed, and I pushed again, my mouth on hers.

We both came, our bodies shaking, and I hovered on top of her, watching as she came down from her orgasm, my thumb sliding along her cheek. I needed to touch her, no matter where we were, what we were doing, I needed to have my hands on her.

Needed to.

"You okay?" I whispered, my voice hoarse.

"I'm wonderful. You give good sex," she said, her eyes dancing.

I leaned down and kissed her lips. "You give good sex too, love." Another kiss. "Let me clean us up, then I'll feed you like I promised."

"Cake?" She grinned and then wiggled.

I rolled my eyes, even as I sucked in a breath. We'd had sex three times over the past few hours and, somehow, she was getting me hard again. This woman. This damned amazing woman. "Maybe."

I slid out of her and then went to clean us up. We were

quiet, taking our time. We'd been together for six months now, and still I learned more and more about her as each moment passed. I couldn't wait to find out more. To discover who *I* was when I was with her.

By the time we were both dressed, at least somewhat, I picked her up by the hips and sat her on the kitchen counter. She crossed her bare legs since she wore only my shirt, and I fed her cake bite by bite, sharing a fork with her.

"You know, I was going to cook for you. Pasta or something."

She grinned around a mouthful of chocolate cake before swallowing the big bite. "We can do that tomorrow."

I shook my head and set down the fork before putting both hands on the counter on either side of her. "Nope. I'm taking you out on a date. It's our anniversary."

She frowned. "Our anniversary is Christmas Eve..."

"Nope. I'm counting this as six months since our first date where I took you to your family's for dinner."

"So is this a beard date, then?" She smiled as she said it, and I couldn't help but taste her lips. Seriously, this woman was addicting.

"It can be if you want. I'll always be your beard." A nip on the lips. "But then again, I'm all real, too."

"Good." She bit my jaw. "I'm needy."

"Just how I like it." I grinned and then went back to feeding her cake.

My phone buzzed, and Amelia picked it up since it was

beside her. "It's Melinda," she said, handing it over. "Everything okay?"

I nodded, looking down at the text. In the past six months, things had changed dramatically, but we were all closer because of it. The two women were friends now, both fighters and advocates for Evan.

During the worst of the treatments, Melinda had come down with pneumonia, and Robbie had asked me and Amelia to help out while he took care of his wife. Since Evan's immune system had almost been nonexistent at that point, Melinda could only see her son through video chats, not in person.

But Amelia had stepped in, along with the rest of the Carrs, and Evan was never alone.

There was never any animosity or weirdness between us. We were all just people who wanted to make sure that Evan was loved, healthy, and whole.

Melinda was a friend now, someone I had a past with, only in that it had brought Evan into our lives.

Robbie was also part of our group now, someone who hung out with me and Devin and the others when he could.

And Evan...Evan was my son.

He still called me "Tucker," and I'd be fine with that for the rest of my life if that's what he wanted. Robbie was his dad. Would always be so. But I was part of his life now, and we were following our own path.

**Melinda:** *Evan says he wants a Mario Kart party for his* *birthday. We're working that out since I thought kids were into different things these days. Want to help?*

I snorted. "Evan picked *Mario Kart* as his party theme."

Amelia threw her fist in the air. "Yes! I knew he'd like that."

"So it was your idea?" I shook my head. "I should have known it was you."

"That kid is a savant when it comes to *Rainbow Road*. He kicks your ass at *Mario Kart*. That's why you're all grumpy now."

"He does not," I grumbled.

**Me**: *We're in. Blame Amelia for the idea.*

**Melinda**: *I should have known! Tell her thanks, though. Robbie's excited. See you on Saturday?*

**Me**: *See you then. Tell the kid I'll call him tomorrow.*

**Melinda**: *Will do.*

I set the phone back down next to Amelia's hip then went back to feeding her cake. "So, Saturday, we're party planning, and then I work a night shift. Sound good?"

"Yep. And then I'm heading out for a girls' night since Zoey has details about a certain thing that no one is talking about."

I raised my brows. "Oh, really?"

"Yup. A certain thing a certain brother isn't talking about either. So, of course, Erin and I are going to grill Zoey for details."

"And you'll tell me when I get home?" I'd moved into

her place the month prior, both of us deciding that moving a greenhouse was out of the question. The house was big enough for both of us, plus Evan had a room here as well in case he ever wanted to spend the night. He hadn't yet, but now that his treatments were doing their thing and he was allowed to be at home, he came over once a week and sometimes napped in his room.

As a kid, I'd never had a true room of my own. I wanted my son to have his own space, even if he wasn't here often.

"Of course," she said, dancing a bit from her seat. "Should be interesting."

Thinking about the fact that the family always wanted to know what Amelia and I were up to, I wasn't so sure. I was giving Caleb and Zoey a wide berth when it came to whatever the hell those two were doing.

After all, I had my own life to work through. But at least I wasn't alone.

I'd never be alone again, not with the family I'd made from bonds, not blood. And the woman in front of me.

"I love you," I whispered, lowering my head to hers.

She smiled sweetly, her eyes warm. "I love you, too. You're the best fake date I've ever had."

"And you're the best real date I'll ever need."

And when we kissed again, we forgot all about the cake, about other people's problems, and only had eyes for each other.

I'd fallen in love with my best friend's little sister. The most reckless thing I'd ever done.

But I knew I'd do it again in a heartbeat.

THE END

Next in the Less Than series?

It's Zoe and Caleb's turn in SHAMELESS WITH HIM.

**Want to read a special BONUS EPILOGUE featuring Amelia and Tucker? CLICK HERE!**

# A NOTE FROM CARRIE ANN RYAN

Thank you so much for reading **RECKLESS WITH YOU.** I do hope if you liked this story, that you would please leave a review!

I adored writing this book. I knew all along Amelia would end up with Tucker. Falling for your brother's best friend is my favorite trope after all. But when Tobey showed up, I knew something was odd about him. So yes, this isn't the book where you fall for your best friend and it works. I've written those before. This is the book where you make a mistake, then realize what's right for you in the end.

As for who is next? Caleb and Zoe finally figure things out in Shameless With Him. Well, at least I hope so!

**The Less Than Series:**
Book 1: Breathless With Her

Book 2: Reckless With You

Book 3: Shameless With Him

## WANT TO READ A SPECIAL BONUS EPILOGUE FEATURING AMELIA AND TUCKER? CLICK HERE!

If you want to make sure you know what's coming next from me, you can sign up for my newsletter at www. CarrieAnnRyan.com; follow me on twitter at @CarrieAnnRyan, or like my Facebook page. I also have a Facebook Fan Club where we have trivia, chats, and other goodies. You guys are the reason I get to do what I do and I thank you.

Make sure you're signed up for my MAILING LIST so you can know when the next releases are available as well as find giveaways and FREE READS.

Happy Reading!

# Also from Carrie Ann Ryan

**The Montgomery Ink Legacy Series:**
Book 1: Bittersweet Promises

**The Wilder Brothers Series:**
Book 1: One Way Back to Me
Book 2: Always the One for Me

**The Aspen Pack Series:**
Book 1: Etched in Honor

**The Montgomery Ink: Fort Collins Series:**
Book 1: Inked Persuasion
Book 2: Inked Obsession
Book 3: Inked Devotion

Book 3.5: Nothing But Ink

Book 4: Inked Craving

Book 5: Inked Temptation

**The Montgomery Ink: Boulder Series:**

Book 1: Wrapped in Ink

Book 2: Sated in Ink

Book 3: Embraced in Ink

Book 3: Moments in Ink

Book 4: Seduced in Ink

Book 4.5: Captured in Ink

Book 4.7: Inked Fantasy

Book 4.8: A Very Montgomery Christmas

**Montgomery Ink: Colorado Springs**

Book 1: Fallen Ink

Book 2: Restless Ink

Book 2.5: Ashes to Ink

Book 3: Jagged Ink

Book 3.5: Ink by Numbers

**Montgomery Ink Denver:**

Book 0.5: Ink Inspired

Book 0.6: Ink Reunited

Book 1: Delicate Ink

Book 1.5: Forever Ink

Book 2: Tempting Boundaries

Book 3: Harder than Words
Book 3.5: Finally Found You
Book 4: Written in Ink
Book 4.5: Hidden Ink
Book 5: Ink Enduring
Book 6: Ink Exposed
Book 6.5: Adoring Ink
Book 6.6: Love, Honor, & Ink
Book 7: Inked Expressions
Book 7.3: Dropout
Book 7.5: Executive Ink
Book 8: Inked Memories
Book 8.5: Inked Nights
Book 8.7: Second Chance Ink
Book 8.5: Montgomery Midnight Kisses
Bonus: Inked Kingdom

**The On My Own Series:**
Book 0.5: My First Glance
Book 1: My One Night
Book 2: My Rebound
Book 3: My Next Play
Book 4: My Bad Decisions

**The Promise Me Series:**
Book 1: Forever Only Once
Book 2: From That Moment

Book 3: Far From Destined

Book 4: From Our First

**The Less Than Series:**

Book 1: Breathless With Her

Book 2: Reckless With You

Book 3: Shameless With Him

**The Fractured Connections Series:**

Book 1: Breaking Without You

Book 2: Shouldn't Have You

Book 3: Falling With You

Book 4: Taken With You

**The Whiskey and Lies Series:**

Book 1: Whiskey Secrets

Book 2: Whiskey Reveals

Book 3: Whiskey Undone

**The Gallagher Brothers Series:**

Book 1: Love Restored

Book 2: Passion Restored

Book 3: Hope Restored

**The Ravenwood Coven Series:**

Book 1: Dawn Unearthed

Book 2: Dusk Unveiled

Book 3: Evernight Unleashed

**The Talon Pack:**
 Book 1: Tattered Loyalties
 Book 2: An Alpha's Choice
 Book 3: Mated in Mist
 Book 4: Wolf Betrayed
 Book 5: Fractured Silence
 Book 6: Destiny Disgraced
 Book 7: Eternal Mourning
 Book 8: Strength Enduring
 Book 9: Forever Broken
 Book 10: Mated in Darkness
 Book 11: Fated in Winter

**Redwood Pack Series:**
 Book 1: An Alpha's Path
 Book 2: A Taste for a Mate
 Book 3: Trinity Bound
 Book 3.5: A Night Away
 Book 4: Enforcer's Redemption
 Book 4.5: Blurred Expectations
 Book 4.7: Forgiveness
 Book 5: Shattered Emotions
 Book 6: Hidden Destiny
 Book 6.5: A Beta's Haven
 Book 7: Fighting Fate

Book 7.5: <u>Loving the Omega</u>
Book 7.7: <u>The Hunted Heart</u>
Book 8: <u>Wicked Wolf</u>

**The Elements of Five Series:**
Book 1: From Breath and Ruin
Book 2: From Flame and Ash
Book 3: From Spirit and Binding
Book 4: From Shadow and Silence

**Dante's Circle Series:**
Book 1: <u>Dust of My Wings</u>
Book 2: <u>Her Warriors' Three Wishes</u>
Book 3: <u>An Unlucky Moon</u>
Book 3.5: <u>His Choice</u>
Book 4: <u>Tangled Innocence</u>
Book 5: <u>Fierce Enchantment</u>
Book 6: <u>An Immortal's Song</u>
Book 7: <u>Prowled Darkness</u>
Book 8: Dante's Circle Reborn

**Holiday, Montana Series:**
Book 1: <u>Charmed Spirits</u>
Book 2: <u>Santa's Executive</u>
Book 3: <u>Finding Abigail</u>
Book 4: <u>Her Lucky Love</u>
Book 5: Dreams of Ivory

**The Branded Pack Series:**
**(Written with Alexandra Ivy)**
Book 1: <u>Stolen and Forgiven</u>
Book 2: <u>Abandoned and Unseen</u>
Book 3: <u>Buried and Shadowed</u>

# ABOUT THE AUTHOR

Carrie Ann Ryan is the New York Times and USA Today bestselling author of contemporary, paranormal, and young adult romance. Her works include the Montgomery Ink, Redwood Pack, Fractured Connections, and Elements of Five series, which have sold over 3.0 million books worldwide. She started writing while in graduate school for her advanced degree in chemistry and hasn't stopped since.

Carrie Ann has written over seventy-five novels and novellas with more in the works. When she's not losing herself in her emotional and action-packed worlds, she's reading as much as she can while wrangling her clowder of cats who have more followers than she does.

www.CarrieAnnRyan.com